"Stop practicing your seduction techniques on me..."

Eric leaned in, doing his best to ignore Julie's delicious scent, and waited until she looked at him.

"Have you considered that I am not a nice guy? That I'm actually the kind of man your mother warned you about?"

Julie's eyelashes flickered as if the thought hadn't occurred to her. "Not possible. You would never take advantage of a good girl like me."

He stared into her eyes. Was she playing him? Or was she really that innocent?

She winked.

He wanted to growl. Give her a taste of the intense sexual need warring inside him. Instead, he pushed away from her cubicle and strode off. "Don't test your luck with me or you will find out just what kind of man I really am."

Her husky laugh followed him. "I'm looking forward to it...."

Dear Reader,

I have always enjoyed detective shows that combine mystery with romance and comedy. Give me a hero and heroine who must work closely together while trying to resist a powerful attraction and I will tune in every time! I want to watch the couple gradually fall in love and see how each mystery tests and strengthens their relationship. My only complaint is that many of these shows tease the viewers with red-hot scenarios but they don't deliver the sizzle.

The lack of heat in some of my favorite detective shows was what inspired me to write this story. I wanted to watch a detective show that was fun, sexy and romantic. Something that offered the same experience as the Harlequin Blaze novels I read. I started to wonder how I would give a detective story the Blaze treatment. The result is *Suddenly Sexy*.

Thanks for reading Julie and Eric's story. Don't forget to visit my website, susannacarr.com, for news, excerpts, contests and more.

Enjoy!

Susanna Carr

Susanna Carr

SUDDENLY SEXY

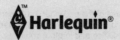

TORONTO NEW YORK LONDON
AMSTERDAM PARIS SYDNEY HAMBURG
STOCKHOLM ATHENS TOKYO MILAN MADRID
PRAGUE WARSAW BUDAPEST AUCKLAND

Recycling programs for this product may not exist in your area.

ISBN-13: 978-0-373-79696-0

SUDDENLY SEXY

Copyright © 2012 by Jasmine Communications, LLC

All rights reserved. Except for use in any review, the reproduction or utilization of this work in whole or in part in any form by any electronic, mechanical or other means, now known or hereafter invented, including xerography, photocopying and recording, or in any information storage or retrieval system, is forbidden without the written permission of the publisher, Harlequin Enterprises Limited, 225 Duncan Mill Road, Don Mills, Ontario M3B 3K9, Canada.

This is a work of fiction. Names, characters, places and incidents are either the product of the author's imagination or are used fictitiously, and any resemblance to actual persons, living or dead, business establishments, events or locales is entirely coincidental.

This edition published by arrangement with Harlequin Books S.A.

For questions and comments about the quality of this book please contact us at Customer_eCare@Harlequin.ca.

® and TM are trademarks of the publisher. Trademarks indicated with ® are registered in the United States Patent and Trademark Office, the Canadian Trade Marks Office and in other countries.

www.Harlequin.com

Printed in U.S.A.

ABOUT THE AUTHOR

Susanna Carr lives in the Pacific Northwest with her family. When she isn't writing, Susanna enjoys reading romance and connecting with readers online. Visit her website at susannacarr.com.

To Kathryn Lye and Jenny Bent, with thanks

1

BAD GIRLS HAD ALL THE FUN.

Julie Kent scowled with envy and slammed her book closed. She exhaled sharply as frustration swelled inside her until it felt as if it would burst through her skin. It was probably wrong that she wanted to be like the villainess in the *Sex, Spies and Sapphires* espionage series, even if the villainess was the main character. Sapphire was sexy, aggressive, kick-ass and daring. She was also a thief. Not to mention fictional.

Julie still wouldn't mind being a bit more like Sapphire and a little less...Julie. She wanted to break the rules. Break a sweat. Take risks. Take on the world and a few men while she was at it. Sapphire managed to have sex with more men in this book than Julie had in her lifetime.

And this was just one book in a whole series. Julie sighed and dropped the paperback in her bottom desk drawer. She kicked the drawer shut and propped her chin on her hand. She wasn't asking to have lots of sex with lots of guys. Treating beds as merry-go-rounds wasn't for her, not that she had any opportunity to treat them as such. She just wanted lots of sex with one guy: Eric Ranger.

Julie turned her head and peered over her gray cubicle, staring at Eric's closed office door. She bit her bottom lip as she recalled every inch of the man's lean muscular build. Eric moved with a lethal grace that she found mesmerizing. She bet he could guide her through some of the steamy scenes she'd just read, and come up with a few imaginative positions that would give her maximum pleasure.

"Julie?"

Julie stifled a shriek and whirled around in her chair. Her friend Asia was leaning on the cubicle wall. She smiled knowingly as she drummed her perfectly manicured nails on the cubicle frame. How long had she been standing there?

"We need to work on your observation skills," Asia teased.

"Sorry, I was daydreaming." Julie felt the blush heating her cheeks.

"Yeah, I have a pretty good idea who was starring in that dream." Asia slapped the cubicle with her hand. "One of these days you need to stop fantasizing and just go for it."

Julie simply nodded. Her friend always gave her this kind of well-meaning advice, but she didn't understand that they operated under different sets of rules. Asia was drop-dead gorgeous and had the confidence of an action hero. The two traits went hand in hand. The woman strutted through life, knowing she could get any man she wanted.

Julie, on the other hand, could strive for "pretty" on a good day. She was used to being overlooked by men, especially when she hung out with Asia. It was fine. Sometimes she liked to believe that the right guy would be instantly attracted to her without any work on her part, but who was she kidding? A man like Eric could be effortlessly sexy in jeans and a T-shirt, but a woman like herself needed all the help she could get.

"So, what brings you to my little cubicle?" Julie asked. She wasn't even peripherally involved with Asia's cases and their lunch break had just ended.

"The boss says Eric isn't answering his phone or IM. I thought you might like to see if he's in his office," Asia said, wagging her eyebrows suggestively. "Everyone is supposed to meet in the conference room in ten minutes."

"I'll get him." She was glad for any excuse to talk to Eric, and she appreciated her friend's help.

"Unless you're busy," Asia said as she strolled away.

Julie rolled her eyes. "That'll be the day." She stood up and headed for Eric's door. Busy. Right. She knew her hometown wasn't the center for international espionage or criminal activity. Close to Seattle, Redmond was a quiet, suburban city known for Microsoft and which claimed to be the bicycle capital of the northwest. Julie had more of a chance to bump into a computer nerd or cyclist than a crook. Yet when she joined Gunthrie Security & Investigations, she had dreams of high-speed chases, death-defying maneuvers and breathtaking excitement as she saved the world while earning an edgy, cool nickname.

She got a nickname all right. Uniform Girl. From

eight to four-thirty Monday to Friday she kept track of the uniforms for their security guards assigned all around the Seattle area.

So much for her crime-fighting career. Perry Gunthrie was a sweet old man who truly felt her job was important. And it probably was to Gunthrie S&I. Times were tough and the investigation cases were not plentiful. The security contracts were barely keeping them afloat.

But Eric Ranger was going to change all that. Julie had no doubt that he would succeed, even if he was only going to be around for a few more weeks until his medical leave was up. Eric didn't talk a lot about his job, but Julie had learned that he worked for the Cultural Property, Art and Antiquities Program under the Immigration and Custom Enforcement agency. ICE. She loved that acronym. It sounded very James Bond to her. Eric's job was to find stolen artwork and historical artifacts and return them to their rightful owners. Eric got injured while on an ICE assignment in Muscat, wherever that was. It sounded exotic and exciting to Julie. She would bet her paycheck that he'd gotten hurt from taking down a criminal mastermind.

Julie sighed. Some guys have all the fun.

Now he was helping Perry, his godfather, while on a leave of absence. When Julie had first heard that after meeting him, her tongue almost rolled out and landed on the floor. She couldn't get her last boyfriend to give up a Saturday to help her move, but Eric dropped everything and flew across the country from D.C. to Seattle to help out a friend of the family. There had to be something wrong with this guy that she hadn't figured out. However, if there were, she really didn't want to know.

Doing a favor for Perry hadn't been a vacation for Eric. For the past six weeks he had done everything he could to gain more clients. There had been lots of meetings with companies, lots of crunching numbers and lots of sleepless nights. Julie had never seen anyone work that hard. She had tried to show her support and unofficially looked after Eric behind the scenes. She didn't think she was much help, and she didn't get any tips on how to act like a special agent, either. But she still had a few more weeks to study Eric, inch by glorious inch, before he returned to Washington, D.C.

Julie paused in front of his small office and brushed her fingers through her straight brown hair. She lightly tapped on the door. "Eric?"

Nothing.

She knocked harder. "Eric? It's Julie." Hmm, he probably didn't remember her name, but she refused to call herself Uniform Girl.

Still no answer. He probably wasn't in his office. Eric might be out taking a million-mile jog or leaping tall buildings for a little cardio workout. She should try to emulate him if she wanted to be a kick-ass detective, but she could barely get through her aerobics class without wanting to die.

Julie tried the doorknob and it moved under her hand. She slowly opened the door and found the room dark. "Eric?"

She peered around the door and froze as her heart lurched. Eric Ranger was asleep, sprawled out on the tattered couch, wearing nothing but a pair of black boxer briefs.

Whoa. Julie's mind started to shut down as she stared at his masculine beauty. Her heart started to race. She studied each slope and angle of his sculpted chest and flat abdomen. Eric was lean and muscular. She felt his power even though he lay sprawled on the couch.

The jagged scar on his side caught her gaze. It was long, deep and an angry red. As she watched him sleep, Julie realized there were quite a few marks scoring his golden skin. On his hands, his legs and the bottom of his feet. Some of them looked decades old. This was the body of a warrior. This was a man who had seen the rough and brutal side of life.

Julie gripped the doorknob and hesitated. She knew the polite thing to do would be to close the door and pound on it until he woke up. But she wanted to stare and memorize every line. No, that wasn't quite true. She wanted to touch him. Stroke him. Curl up next to Eric and feel the power and strength of his body as she slowly woke him up.

But she would keep her hands to herself. Because she was too much of a good girl, damn it. She vaguely wondered what Sapphire would do in this situation.

Sapphire would probably tackle him. Okay, maybe not right away. First she would tie him down, tease and torment him until he begged for release. And then Sapphire would straddle Eric before licking every inch of him.

Julie swiped her tongue along her bottom lip as her mouth tingled with anticipation. *Noooo...* Julie pressed her tongue firmly against the roof of her mouth. Why was she even thinking about it? She'd never do that in a million years, no matter how much she wanted to.

She heard the squeaky metal of a chair from behind her. Julie looked over her shoulder and noticed the other employees were heading toward the conference room. She needed to stop hanging back and wake up Eric before someone came looking for both of them.

She took a deep breath and stepped into Eric's tiny office, dodged a pile of clothes on the floor and firmly closed the door. Heat tingled along her skin, stung with awareness. She needed to control the excitement stirring deep in her belly.

Julie smoothed her hands against her turquoise blue wrap dress and nervously cleared her throat. She might not have the courage to sweep her tongue along Eric's golden skin, but she could act like she saw practically naked hot guys every day.

Just not ones who were that ripped.

"Eric," she said in a brisk I-am-so-not-looking-at-your-boxers tone. "You need to get up. The meeting is about to start."

Nothing. He didn't move.

"You know," she said a little louder, "the meeting you're supposed to lead. The one about our future at Gunthrie S and I."

Still nothing.

She reached out and tentatively tapped his shoulder. Wow. The guy was muscular. His skin was warm and smooth. She reluctantly pulled her hand away. "Eric?"

He still didn't move. Julie frowned. That couldn't be good. Did he always sleep this soundly? Special agents were supposed to be light sleepers, ready to shoot and kill the moment they heard footsteps. Everyone who reads espionage novels knew that. If they didn't get up, they were dead, drugged or in a coma until the next book came out.

She studied Eric's sleeping form. He was motionless, his broad, sculpted chest barely moving with every breath. Hmm…

Julie leaned over him, her face just above his, and checked for signs of breathing. "Eric?" she whispered.

Her world suddenly spun. One minute she was standing and the next moment her feet were in the air. Julie cried out as her spine collided against the bristly carpet. Her arms, stretched above her head, were pinned down. Her breath hitched in her throat as a heavy weight descended on her ribs.

She blinked at the sight of Eric's face inches away from hers. Her mouth went dry as she took it all in. His short blond hair was mussed and his dark blue eyes were still blurry with sleep. Whiskers shadowed his angular jaw and she itched to rub her cheek against his.

Eric squeezed his eyes shut, the lines in his face deepening. He opened his eyes again. "Julie?"

He knew her name, she thought dazedly. That was hopeful.

And he wasn't moving away from her. Eric kept her pinned to the floor. His knee was deeply, intimately, wedged between her thighs as his big, muscular, not to mention *naked* chest crushed her breasts.

"How'd you do that?" she asked in a breathless squeak. And could she use that move to flip him into her bed?

Eric jumped to his feet in one fluid movement. He

reached for her, his hands surprisingly gentle. Eric set her on her wobbly feet before she could take her next breath.

"I'm sorry," he said. He pulled his hand away and rubbed the back of his neck. "I didn't mean to do that. Are you okay?"

"I'm fine. No harm done." Except for knowing how it felt to be pressed against his rock-hard body. "I'm supposed to get you for the meeting in the conference room."

"Damn." He looked at his watch. It was a sophisticated timepiece that looked as complicated as the dashboard of a race car. "I'll be right there."

"Take your time," Julie offered as she tugged her dress into place and hurriedly made her way to the door. She felt off balance, as if her world had been thrown off its axis.

"Julie?"

She turned around and kept her eyes firmly above his bare shoulders. It didn't help. Her gaze wandered down to his snug boxer briefs and she started to blush. "Yeah?"

"I didn't mean to scare you."

"Scare me?" She frowned. He thought one accidental tumble scared her? Seriously? What did he think she was made of? Julie thrust her chin out with injured pride. "Eric, the only one who seems freaked out is you."

HE BLEW IT. ERIC GRITTED HIS teeth as the disappointment rolled through him. Six weeks of being a gentleman and he ruined it by one instinctive move. Tackling a woman and pinning her to the floor was not the way to her heart.

Eric hovered over the sink in the men's restroom and sluiced ice-cold water over his face. He regretted falling asleep in the office instead of driving back to his hotel in Bellevue. He was alert now, but it was too late to fix anything. He glanced up and looked in the mirror. He saw the scars along with the weariness and the darkness in his eyes. He was not the knight in shining armor that Julie wanted.

He had spent most of his adult life as a government agent. He was honored to serve his country, although he spent most of his days outside its borders. He missed home, but he had a sense of pride over his accomplishments.

He could also speak three languages, assimilate in any major city and handle a gun and knife with the same ease as a knife and fork. So, why did he feel like a monster around Julie?

Because he was a monster. Eric speared his wet hands through his hair, allowing the water to drip down his head and neck. He had been wild and destructive as a child. His home life had been a battlefield and then a wasteland. When he left home, he had been trained to destroy and shoot to kill. Julie was the opposite. She was creative and saw the good in everyone. She liked her espionage novels and believed that good always won over evil.

Eric didn't remember when he stopped believing in that fairy tale, but he didn't want her to find out the truth. He may be bitter, but he found her sweetness addicting in a way he never understood before. If he got close to her, even touched her, he would taint her with the darkness of his world.

He wasn't going to let that happen. He would do whatever it took to protect her sunny view of the world.

What was it about her that had gotten under his skin? There was something about Julie that made him want to linger around her. She was always smiling, her eyes sparkling with enthusiasm. She had endless energy and an insatiable curiosity.

But there was something about Julie that made him sweat. There was a natural sexiness about her, in the way she walked, in the way she laughed and the way she dressed. At the last casual Friday, Julie had worn a pink tank top, blue jeans and flip-flops. Eric had been so mesmerized that he had found it difficult to concentrate.

And he needed to concentrate right now. Eric wiped the water from his face and gripped the edge of the sink. Today he had to give some bad news to the company. He immediately conjured an image of Julie. She was going to be upset and there was nothing he could do to comfort her. It was just another mark against him.

Eric took a deep breath and straightened to his full height. He wasn't one to procrastinate. He tugged at his shirt collar, checked his watch and headed for the conference room.

The moment he walked into the room, everyone at the table fell into silence.

There were only fifteen people who worked at Gunthrie S&I. Ten of them were only qualified to do the administration work for the security accounts. The remaining employees were licensed investigators.

Ace, a computer nerd who only wore jeans and gaming T-shirts, did computer forensic work. Martha did interviews and surveillance. A grandmotherly type, she often said that she was good at her job because she was practically invisible. Max was retired military and did most of the background checks.

All of these investigators learned on the job with Perry. The only employee who had any real experience was Asia. She had been a police officer and was Gunthrie's top investigator.

Until Eric had shown up. Asia wasn't pleased when he started taking over. Eric knew he had the skills Perry needed right now to keep Gunthrie S&I open for business. He coordinated missions, trained lower-level agents and knew how to represent his work to other organizations and companies.

While working with Perry over the past six weeks, Eric had been giving the older man a crash course in the cutting-edge techniques for conducting criminal investigations. In the past, the latest trends would have excited Perry, but now it made him feel overwhelmed and defeated. When Eric had suggested trying a different kind of investigation, it took a while to convince Perry to give it a try.

Eric saw his godfather sitting at the head of the table and gave him an encouraging smile. Eric automatically searched for Julie.

She was whispering furiously with her friend Asia. As Eric moved to the foot of the table, he considered how strange the friendship was between Asia and Julie. They were an unlikely pair. Asia was shrewd and abrasive while Julie was warm and friendly.

He reluctantly pulled his attention away and noticed the other employees watching him. Did they know everyone was in danger of losing their jobs? They were good people, though some were odder than the others. There were a few he wouldn't trust with a car, let alone a gun. All of the employees seemed to emulate their detective idol, right down to the catchphrases. They made up for their lack of experience and technological know-how with hard work and enthusiasm.

"Okay, everyone," Eric said. "I'm going to just open the meeting with some news. We no longer provide security services for Bellows and Groggins. Murphy and Associates won the bid."

There was a beat of heavy silence. Eric paused to let the news sink in. His attention gravitated toward Julie. He frowned when it registered that she didn't seem particularly worried. In fact, she looked at him as if he would come up with a perfectly good solution to keep the business afloat.

There was something about that look. It was as if she trusted his skills and strategies completely. As if she knew behind the scars and the fatigue, there was a hero inside him ready to save the day.

The way she was looking at him, he almost believed it, too.

He didn't realize he'd allowed the pause to linger for too long. The employees started to all talk at once, their voices beginning to rise with panic and anger.

Eric raised his hands and motioned for them to quiet down. "But this gives us an opportunity to move in a new direction."

He was determined to give the idea a good spin, but

he didn't know how the rest of the office would react. When he ran it by his godfather, Perry was surprised. The sad thing was that it didn't shock Eric at all. He wondered if that was a sign. Was he jaded? Was he that world-weary and cynical?

"Investigations are a lucrative field and Perry has approved of it." Eric didn't feel the need to mention how much convincing it took to get Perry to sign off on the idea. "It will require a lot of man hours so everyone will be assigned cases."

The tension in the room slowly disappeared. He had a feeling it would. Everyone at Gunthrie S&I wanted to be on a case. They longed to solve puzzles that didn't come out of the crosswords or Sudoku section of the newspaper.

Eric saw Julie sit straight up in her chair. He should have known. Julie has been badgering Perry to let her on a case. Eric saw the thirst for adventure and excitement inside her. It was his job to keep that in control.

"What type of investigation?" Max asked, as he stroked his *Magnum, P.I.* mustache.

Eric paused as he tried to come up with the most professional description. "We are going to provide premarital screenings and decoy assignments."

Max cast a glance at Martha, a Miss Marple look-alike who sat next to him. Max returned a steady gaze at Eric. "You mean we're going to spy on cheating boyfriends?"

Eric gave a deep sigh. So much for trying to make it sound more important. "That's one of way of explaining it."

"And lead them into temptation?" Martha asked.

Eric winced. "Yeah."

"We've never done that before," Max said, his voice tinged with excitement. "Count me in."

Everyone started talking. He heard someone claiming seniority while another insisted his dubious familiarity with nightclubs was necessary for the project.

"I'm proposing we do a trial run," Eric said over the voices and waited for them to quiet down again. "First we will need to put together a surveillance team. Audio, visual…"

A couple of people eagerly put up their hands. Eric assigned them roles best suited for their strengths and weaknesses.

"We need a team to do background checks." Several hands went up. "And we need a decoy," Eric said as he wrote down the names of the volunteers.

"Decoy?" Martha frowned. "What do you mean by that?"

"We need a seductive woman who will put the moves on our target and see if he takes the bait."

"Ooh!" Julie's hand thrust up high. "Pick me!"

A cold chill swept through Eric. No, no, no. Not Julie. She was too innocent, too sweet. He didn't want Julie as a decoy. It could get dangerous.

"She needs to seduce a man who is probably a bastard," Eric said between clenched teeth.

Julie waved her hand wildly. "I can do that!"

"She needs to know self-defense," Eric continued.

Julie propped up her waving arm with her other hand. "I took a course last month."

"Eric," Perry said with wry amusement, "I believe someone is volunteering to become a decoy."

Eric met Julie's gaze. Her eyes glowed and her cheeks were flushed. She radiated with enthusiasm. Julie looked incredibly beautiful and sexy.

He wanted to be the good guy. He wanted to give her everything her heart desired, but he couldn't allow her to take on this assignment. She would discover how emotionally draining it was to pretend all the time and lie convincingly. She would start to see the dark underbelly of her world and she would begin to question why she wanted to save it in the first place.

He wasn't going to be the one who destroyed her innocence. He wanted her to hold on to it just a little while longer.

Eric struggled to break eye contact and looked around the room. "Anyone else?"

2

JULIE FROWNED. WHAT WAS going on? He didn't write down her name. How many decoys did they possibly need? And it wasn't as if he had a vast pool of potential candidates.

"No, seriously, I can do it," she insisted, waving her arm to capture his attention. "I can be the decoy."

Eric didn't look at her. "We'll take that under consideration. Asia? What about you?"

Julie's hand went down with a thump. *Oh...* Of course. Her face started to burn bright red as her stomach did a sickening, spiral dive.

What was she thinking? Asia was gorgeous and glamorous. There was a hint of a challenge and the promise of danger in her eyes that men found irresistible. Asia could lead any man to temptation. Julie couldn't lead a man anywhere even if she had a detailed map.

Asia leaned back in her chair and toyed with a pen in her hands. "Sorry, I would make a horrible decoy, but I'd like to take lead on the trial run."

"Eric will be in charge," Perry kindly informed Asia. "But you would make a great decoy. I know you had practice on the force."

"The focus on those stings was different. We weren't targeting a specific person. Anyway," she said with a shrug of her shoulder, "I don't approach men—they approach me."

Julie silently nodded in agreement. She had seen it countless times. She was sure Asia could approach men with success, but her friend never needed to practice.

"However," Asia continued, "I think Julie would make a great decoy."

"Thanks," Julie said softly as she kept her head down and her gaze firmly on her clenched hands in her lap. She appreciated what her friend was trying to do, but it wasn't any use. She wasn't like Asia. She wasn't even Asia-lite.

Eric exhaled sharply. "We can always hire out an independent contractor."

Ouch. Julie squeezed her eyes closed. Could the humiliation get any worse?

Asia abruptly leaned forward in her chair. "That would be a waste when we have someone right here."

Julie reached out and placed a restraining hand on her friend's arm. "It's okay, Asia," she whispered. "Let it go."

Asia reluctantly backed down and Julie felt her friend's arm shake with the restrained aggression. Julie also found it difficult to stay in her seat for the remainder of the meeting. She knew people were giving her pitying looks, but that didn't sting as much as Eric's firm and swift rejection.

She hunched her shoulders, trying to appear smaller and invisible as the tears pricked the back of her eyes. Julie heard Eric's voice as he outlined the strategy, but she wasn't listening.

What exactly did Eric think she couldn't do? Did he think she couldn't seduce a man? Or was he unsure if she could be helpful in an investigation? Maybe it was both? Julie pressed her lips together as the pain ricocheted in her body.

Okay, so she wasn't hot like Asia. This was not breaking news. She wasn't mysterious or exotic, but she didn't look like a zombie, either. All she needed was to take on a sexy alias and she could be the best decoy Eric had ever seen.

But maybe he thought it was impossible. The guy had seen and done it all while hunting down artifacts. He'd probably bedded gorgeous women across the globe and met his match with the best seductresses who hid important treasures. Julie couldn't compare to that kind of competition.

Julie gave a start when her coworkers got up from their seats. She hadn't noticed the meeting had ended and she watched the others leave the room, buzzing with enthusiasm about their assignments. She was envious, knowing she was probably going to be stuck with a desk job. There was nothing exciting about that, even if she got to work on the case. Why should she be thrilled at being a Bosley when she wanted to be a Charlie's Angel?

She cautiously glanced in Eric's direction and found him watching her. He held her gaze for a moment and she couldn't look away. His blue eyes were stormy and intense. Eric seemed as if he was about to say something. She braced herself. She had no doubt it would be blunt and brutal.

Eric decided against it and set his mouth in a grim line. He walked out of the conference room without saying a word.

Julie sagged against her chair and took a deep breath.

"That could have gone better," Asia muttered.

"Thanks for coming to my defense," Julie said as she patted Asia's arm. "But if you want the decoy assignment, you should go for it."

Asia rolled her eyes. "Oh, please. That is why I quit the police force. They always wanted me to work for Vice and dress up as a hooker when I wanted to solve cases."

It sounded as if they both couldn't get the assignment they wanted because of the way they looked. Julie never thought of it that way. She always assumed her friend eventually got what she wanted, but maybe Asia's appearance was a disadvantage as well as a benefit.

Asia gathered her pen and notebook. "So, what are you going to do now?"

Julie shrugged. "Before or after I crawl into a hole and lick my wounds?"

"Come on, Julie," Asia said with a hint of exasperation in her voice. "There is no need to roll over and play dead at the first sign of opposition."

Julie pointed at the open door. "He thinks I can't be a seductive woman." She hated how her voice hitched in her throat.

"He didn't say that."

"Then he thinks I can't do detective work." That hurt almost just as much.

"He didn't say that, either." Asia leaned her elbow on the back of her chair and gave her a hard, direct look. "In fact, he didn't make any comment whatsoever. It's up to you to face him and find out why he won't let you be a decoy."

"You're right." She obviously wasn't going to be handed a plum assignment just because she asked for it. Life never worked that way. She needed to find out why Eric was against her and show how wrong he was about her abilities.

Asia rose from her seat and gestured to Julie. "So march into his office right now and find out."

Julie nodded as she reluctantly got up from her seat. As much as she wanted the job, she wasn't ready to find out exactly what Eric thought she lacked. The answer was going to be personal. Whatever it was, she didn't think she could put on a brave face and take the criticism on the chin.

Asia crossed her arms and rested her hip on the conference table. "Yeah, go in like that and he'll snowball you."

"Sorry," she said with a wry smile, "my confidence is a little shaken."

But it was more than that. All of her wild and sexy fantasies about Eric died a quick death during the meeting. How many times had she fantasized that he was so overwhelmed with desire that he couldn't control himself? Her daydreams of being a sexy siren to Eric were never going to come true. The reality was a bitter pill to swallow.

"Of course your confidence is shaken. It got knocked around a bit," Asia said. "But you have to appear stronger and more daring than you feel."

"I don't think I can." She was never a fake-it-until-you-make-it kind of person. She was more of a what-you-see-is-what-you-get girl.

"Fine," Asia said. "Then accept Eric's decision with no questions asked and stick to keeping track of uniforms."

Julie shuddered. "Forget that. I want this assignment."

"Good." Asia pointed at the door. "Now go into Eric's office with guns blazing and don't take no for an answer."

Guns blazing. Right. Because that was so how she approached life. "This is going to be a complete waste of time," Julie muttered as she pushed her seat in.

"Show him that you can be just as fierce and tenacious as he is," Asia said with a pump of her fist.

"So he can bodily lift me and toss me out of his office?"

Asia's jaw tightened with annoyance. "If you want to be a decoy, you need to show that you can face any situation and not get rattled when everything goes wrong."

She was absolutely correct. "The police force really lost out when you quit," Julie said as she took a step toward the door.

"Damn right. Now stop stalling and move," Asia ordered as she gave Julie a little push out of the conference room.

ERIC HEARD THE TREAD of her footsteps. They were soft but the stride was determined. He tilted his head back and groaned. He should have remembered that Julie Kent was as stubborn as she was sweet.

At least they could have it out privately. He didn't like shutting her down in front of an audience, but Julie needed to realize that she wasn't ready to be a decoy. Eric rose from behind his desk just as she knocked on his door.

"Come in, Julie."

The door swung open and Julie peeked in. "How'd you know it was me?"

"Lucky guess." He crossed his arms and braced his legs. He was prepared to battle it out with Julie. She needed to know that he was the boss and the expert. She needed to accept his final answer, but he'd show some mercy. The last thing he wanted to do was crush her spirit.

She quickly shut the door and stood in front of his desk. He thought she was a bit nervous, but Julie placed her hands on her hips and met his eyes with a steady stare. "I want to be the decoy."

"Never going to happen."

She blinked at his immediate answer. "Why?"

"Nothing against you, Julie, but you're not the type."

Julie arched one eyebrow. "Care to explain that?"

Eric knew he would have to choose his words very carefully. "You don't have the experience or the edge."

"I've been on the dating scene for a while," she said tightly as she started to tap one foot. "I think I can handle myself quite well."

"That's not what I mean." His gut clenched as he thought about the men Julie dated. They were probably all gentlemen who knew how to treat her like a princess. He wouldn't be able to compete with that. Eric viciously pushed the thought aside. "I'm sure the guys you dated were no match for you, but we're going after a different type."

"No match for me? What are you trying to say? That I date a bunch of spineless computer geeks?"

He was making this worse. Eric decided to sidestep that question. "The decoy candidate needs to think fast when she's trying to entrap a man."

"And she can only do that when she has the proper training and experience?"

"That's right."

Julie tossed her hands in the air with frustration. "But how can I get experience if no one will let me on an assignment?"

"That's not my problem."

"What if you give me on-the-job training?" she asked, her eyes lighting up with enthusiasm. "You can teach me everything I need to know."

Teach her how to seduce a man? Aw, hell, no. That idea had all the markings of a disaster. But it didn't stop him from imagining just how he would tutor her in the art of seduction. He blinked away the image of him caressing her soft, bare skin. "Still not going to happen," he said gruffly.

"I'll do it for free," she offered recklessly.

If he was any kind of businessman, he would consider that offer. Gunthrie S&I had serious money problems, and they could use all the discounts and freebies that came their way. But this was Julie. He wasn't going to risk her neck to save a few bucks.

"If you want to be a part of the investigation, then you can help with coordinating tasks."

"A desk job?" She groaned and made a face. "Come on, Eric. I'm at a desk all day. I want to get out in the field. I want some action."

"The coordinator assignment is all I can offer you." It was the only job where she wouldn't be at risk. It was the only job where he wouldn't have to worry about her. "You're a rookie and you could compromise our cases."

"That's a bunch of bull." Julie glared at him. "You're talking about hiring independent contractors. It's not like you can call a temp agency and ask them to send over decoys. What would their qualifications be?"

He should have seen this coming. He could lie and say they needed to know hand-to-hand combat, but he knew the truth would eventually come out. He might as well get it over with. "They have to be intelligent, seductive and, above all, cautious."

Julie's bottom jaw shifted to one side as if she was struggling to control her temper. "So, they have to be smart and sexy."

There was an awkward beat. "And cautious," Eric added.

"You don't think I fit those requirements?" she asked in a soft, dangerous tone.

"Julie, a lot can go wrong," he said as he rounded his desk and approached her. "Sometimes a guy can sense he's being set up. A paranoid guy is unpredictable."

"Answer the question, Eric."

"You are far too innocent for that kind of work," he said. "I'm not letting you in the field at all."

"Innocent?" Julie said the word in a squawk. As if she were offended by the description.

"You see the good in everyone, which is a great trait," he quickly assured her, "but it's no good when you're investigating."

"I can read people pretty well," she told him.

"What if he goes on the attack?" Eric asked.

"That's unlikely. And, even if it did happen, I took self-defense training."

He remembered her claim. "A one-day lesson?"

Julie's eyes gleamed with anger. "No."

"A weekend course?"

Her mouth tightened. "Maybe."

Eric shook his head. "That's not good enough."

"Wanna bet?"

He had a feeling she was going to say that, and he acted swiftly. He grabbed her arm and twisted her around. With an economy of motions, he wrapped his arm around her neck and pinned her against him before she could squeak out a complaint.

"Hey, this isn't fair." Julie tugged at his arm, but he wasn't going to let go. He knew he wasn't hurting her, only making her uncomfortable. And maybe a little humble.

"How much are we betting?" he asked.

She wiggled against him as she tried to shove an elbow in his stomach and ribs. Her blows were feeble, but his good intentions were weakening by the way her ass rubbed against his groin.

Julie reached blindly for his face, possibly to claw at him, but it wasn't going to work. "Are you attacking me or trying to get DNA samples for when the coroner inspects your dead, lifeless body?"

She grunted and went for his instep. She tried to stomp on his foot, but he moved the moment he felt her leg muscles bunch. Even if she had managed to get lucky, her ballet slippers wouldn't have caused much damage.

"This isn't proving anything," she muttered as she made a wild swing for who only knew which part of his body. "You are trained to take a man down in a sleeper hold. Not many guys are around here."

"You don't know that." He let her go abruptly.

Julie smoothed her hair and tugged at her dress before turning around. "The chances of a guy getting rough are slim."

"What universe are you living in?" And what kind of guys did she hang around with? Probably computer geeks who only got rough in first-person-shooter video games.

"And even if my target did get rough," Julie continued, "I wouldn't be in some dark, deserted alley with him. You would also have audio and visuals on me."

"That's not enough security. There would be too much of a time lapse before we could get to you."

Julie bunched her hands into fists at her sides and took a deep breath. "I want to be a decoy."

"I said no." She could keep saying it, and he would give her the same answer. "And knowing your aptitude for self-defense, my alternate answer is not in this lifetime."

"Fine." She turned and headed for the door. "I'll just have a little chat with Perry."

"No way." Eric was there, flattening his hand against the door so she couldn't open it.

"He won't say no," Julie informed him as she tugged at the doorknob.

That was what he was worried about. Perry had a soft spot where Julie was concerned. "He's not in charge of this. I am."

Julie hesitated, as if she were trying to come up with a new tactic. She let go of the doorknob and slowly, almost reluctantly, turned around.

When she tilted up her face, her lips were just inches away from his. A tremor swept through his body as his mouth went dry. He was very tempted to brush his mouth against hers. Taste her sweetness and feel her soften against him.

"Tell me the real reason why you won't let me be a decoy. Do you think I'm smart and sexy?" she said in a low tone. She looked him in the eye and then her gaze skittered away.

This was dangerous territory. "I think you're reckless," he answered gruffly. He'd seen how she would jump into a project with unrestrained enthusiasm.

Her eyes gleamed with determination. "I can be cautious."

Eric rolled his eyes.

"And I can do sexy."

Just the way her voice got rough was sexy as hell. His body tightened with anticipation. "But you can't seduce a man." He wasn't going to let her seduce a stranger. Not on his watch.

"Yes, I can."

Eric shook his head. "And you're not the type who

could seduce a man you're not interested in. You're too honest."

Julie thrust out her chin and narrowed her eyes. Why was she taking offense over that statement? "I can seduce anyone when I set my mind to it."

Eric lifted his hands as if he were surrendering. "I'll take your word for it, but you still don't get the job."

She pressed a finger against his chest. "I could seduce you if I wanted to."

The room suddenly went quiet. Eric's muscles locked as the blood roared through his veins. He wanted to take that as an invitation, but he knew Julie didn't mean it that way. He swallowed roughly. "Do you want to?"

The tension arced and shimmered between them. It coiled around them, drawing tighter and tighter until he thought it would spring wildly.

Julie dropped her hand and the tension shattered. She took a step away and winced when she bumped against the door. "For a chance to become a decoy?" she asked in a high voice. "Sure."

Eric took a deep breath as the heavy disappointment pulled at him. Of course she wouldn't go after a guy like him, unless it was to prove something. "You plan to seduce me to show you can be a decoy?"

She crossed her arms protectively in front of her. "I think that should give me enough qualification."

What was that supposed to mean? Eric studied her expression, but he couldn't get a good read. Did she think he was a hard catch, or did she think he was some kind of man-whore? He didn't think he wanted to know. "But I know what you would be up to," he pointed out.

She gave an arrogant shrug. "That will make my seduction of you all the more successful."

Eric could see that Julie was giving this proposal serious consideration. This was bad. This was real bad. He was torn with wanting her to give it her best shot and wanting to get out of target range. "Forget it," he said angrily. "This is ridiculous."

"My seducing you is ridiculous?" She placed her hands on her hips and glared at him. "That's it. I'm taking the challenge. If I can seduce you, I get to be the decoy. Deal?"

"No way." He'd rather make a deal with the devil.

Julie gave him a knowing smile as her eyes shone with defiance. "Because you think I could be successful."

He tried to scoff at her statement, but he wasn't sure if he'd pulled it off. He had to get her out of this mindset. For both their sakes.

"I have known women who have been trained in the erotic arts," he said through gritted teeth. "They are experts at seducing a man and they never got close with me."

"So, I'm not in their league, and you think you have nothing to worry about. Then why are you stalling?" she taunted. "Do we have a deal or not?"

She wasn't going to quit, not even when he hired a few independent contractors. He had to call her bluff. She might make a clumsy move and he would restrain himself long enough to gently rebuff her. He could do this, knowing the other option was allowing her to walk into the jaws of danger.

"If it will get you to shut up about this, then sure."
Eric gripped her outstretched hand, and gave it a firm,
quick shake. "It's a deal."

3

"HAVE YOU LOST YOUR MIND?" Asia asked an hour later as they stood in the women's restroom.

Julie rubbed her forehead with the tips of her fingers, warding off a headache. "I'm beginning to think I have."

"It's an unwritten rule." Asia continued to pace the floor of the small room, the sound of her heels echoing against the tiles. "You never give a guy a heads-up that you're going to seduce him."

"I know, I know." She had been impulsive, but she needed to prove to Eric that she was smart and sexy enough for the job. But she wasn't sure if she *could* pull it off. Flirting was one thing, but she'd never seduced a man before.

Asia covered her face with her hands and took a deep breath. "Okay, we can still make this work." She dropped her hands and studied Julie's appearance with such intensity that Julie wanted to hunch her shoulders and take cover.

"Here's the plan," Asia announced, holding her hands

up high. "Tonight you'll come over to my place and we'll do a makeover. I have some dresses that will drive any guy wild."

"Thanks, Asia, but I don't think that's going to work."

"Why not?"

"We aren't the same size." Asia was a sleek Amazon while she was short and curvy. "And I don't think I can pull off the leather-pants look."

"Don't knock it until you try it."

Julie wished she could try it, but she was pretty sure Asia's leather pants wouldn't go past her ankles. "Anyway, the minute Eric sees me in your clothes he'll know the game's begun."

"That's true. Okay, we're back to square one."

Julie stared at her reflection in the bathroom mirror. "What was I thinking?" she muttered.

She studied her face. It was just another face. Blue eyes, average nose, pink lips. Nothing memorable. Nothing that a man would start a war over or throw his perfectly good life away so he could see it every day.

Her hair was shoulder-length, brown and straight. Big deal. Her body... Julie turned away from the mirror. It was as good as it was going to get.

"Don't let what one guy says make you quit," Asia advised as she patted Julie's shoulder. "You have always wanted to work on a case."

"Yeah, but Eric Ranger isn't just some random guy on the street. He knows what he's talking about."

"Bull. Eric might be an expert when it comes to tracking down a criminal, but he doesn't know every secret a woman has. He doesn't know what you are capable of doing."

"True." But she had a feeling that Eric had met many women just like her. She wouldn't be able to take him by surprise.

"And if he can't see what's so great about you," Asia continued, "than he doesn't deserve you."

There was nothing great about her. She was ordinary.

"But I'm telling you, Julie, he does know."

Julie's mouth twisted in a wry smile. "That's wishful thinking."

"Give my deductive skills some credit," Asia insisted. "I see the way he looks at you. The way he acts. He tries to be the perfect gentleman around you."

"I don't want a gentleman," Julie replied in a low, forceful tone. "I want a hot-blooded man."

"Maybe he thinks you're too ladylike or delicate for the likes of him." Asia shrugged. "It's your job to prove him wrong."

There was that word again. Delicate. She had been delicate when she was growing up, spending so much time at the doctor's office and in bed. She was stronger and healthier now. She didn't want her childhood to define her.

"I want him to see me as strong and powerful." Julie narrowed her eyes as she saw the image before her. "I want him to think I'm so sexy that he's afraid he's going to lose control. I want to be a danger to his sanity, to his heart. And I want him to know that I know it, too."

"Yeah, that sounds like your fantasy woman. What's his fantasy?"

"Huh?"

Asia hesitated as she studied Julie's appearance

again. "I think we're approaching this all wrong. Seduction is about fantasy."

"Keep talking."

"If you want to seduce Eric," Asia said as she rearranged Julie's hair to flow past her shoulders, "you need to create a fantasy. *His* fantasy, not yours."

"I have to become his fantasy girl," Julie murmured as she looked in the mirror again. "Who would be Eric's fantasy girl?"

"That's difficult to say," Asia admitted. "He's been around the world. He's seen and done it all."

"That isn't helping my confidence." Julie tilted her head as she noted her reflection. "I bet Eric's fantasy girl is sleek and glamorous. She wears lots of black and probably has a knife tucked in her garter belt."

Asia scoffed. "Please, you are not dressing up like that character in those books you read."

Huh. She didn't realize she'd described the way Sapphire appeared on the cover of the current book. "You don't think I could pull it off?"

"Eric probably works all day with women like that. His fantasy girl would be someone unattainable. You think your looks are common, but you might be exotic to someone like Eric."

"Oh, I wish." Julie made a face. "You're just saying that because the girl next door is the one look I can pull off."

"I'm telling the truth," Asia said as she caught Julie's gaze in the mirror. "Stop thinking about the woman you wish you were and play up to your strengths."

Julie bit her bottom lip as she considered the strengths of a girl next door. She never thought of them as such.

She could be straightforward without being sexually aggressive. She wasn't particularly thrilled with her wholesome image, but if she tried to approach him as a seductress, he would be on guard.

"I'm going to seduce him. Right now. He won't suspect me making a move so fast." And she won't have time to talk herself out of her plans.

"Go for it!" Asia exclaimed.

"I'll need to disarm him somehow, so I can get close."

"Now you're talking!"

Julie headed for the door. "I need to find the medicine cabinet."

"Whoa!" Asia stopped her by grabbing her arm. "Are we talking disarming or drugging?"

"Don't worry, Asia," Julie said as she gave a comforting pat on her friend's hand. "I want Eric to be fully alert and functioning when I seduce his brains out."

ERIC BARELY HEARD THE timid knock. He dragged his eyes from the computer screen and glared at his office door. He didn't want to see anyone right now. He wasn't in the best mood, and he still had a job to do. "Come in," he said harshly.

When the door opened, Eric was surprised to see Julie peek in. She seemed almost too shy to enter.

"I thought you might need these." In one hand was a cup of water. In the other was a packet of aspirin.

"How did you know?" He knew it was a peace offering. That was totally Julie. She was sweet and nurturing. She also wasn't the type to stay angry for long.

Julie stepped into the office and closed the door with

her elbow. "I shouldn't have carried on like I did," she said with a grimace. "I'm sorry. You have enough to deal with."

"It's okay." Eric slowly began to relax. Julie wasn't going to make another argument to become a decoy. She wasn't going to attempt to seduce him. He admitted he was slightly disappointed in that, but it was for the best.

Everything was all right now. Julie had finally come to her senses. "I want you to know that I wasn't trying to hurt your feelings," he said.

"I understand." Julie placed the water and aspirin packet next to his phone. She rested her hip against the edge of his desk, her leg almost grazing his. "You're protecting me."

Eric frowned. Did her mouth tighten with annoyance? Nah. It was a trick of the light.

"If you want to work on the case, I can have you help out with audio," Eric said. He knew she wanted to feel as if she were part of the team. It was the best compromise he could offer.

"Thanks, I appreciate that." Julie crossed her legs and he heard the rasp of fabric. The turquoise wrap dress tightened against her hips and thighs, emphasizing her curves. He couldn't help but notice her legs were bare and smooth.

Julie tilted her head. "You haven't been getting enough sleep, have you?"

Her question gave him a start. He didn't need a lot of sleep, but lately he had been spending more nights in the office than usual. "What makes you say that?"

Julie leaned closer. The *V* of her neckline gaped

slightly, offering a glimpse of cleavage. "You look really pale."

"I do?" He dragged his gaze from her neckline.

She reached out and flattened her hand against his forehead. Every muscle in his body locked in response. "I don't think you have a fever," she said softly.

Her hand felt good. It was warm and gentle. He imagined what it would be like if she stroked him with those hands. She could torment him with a light touch.

"I can't tell," she said.

"What?" He blinked as he tried to refocus. "Can't tell what?"

"If you have a fever. Hold on." To his surprise, she leaned forward and pressed her mouth against his forehead. His heart lurched at the touch of her lips against his skin.

She was so close. Too close. Eric swiped his tongue along his mouth as he stared at her throat. He wanted to lick every inch of it, and then he would brand her with a love bite so everyone would know she was his.

He shouldn't think like that. Julie wasn't his and never would be. Eric closed his eyes, but that didn't help. He caught a hint of her scent. It was warm and sweet like cinnamon. He found it difficult to swallow.

"No, no fever," she said and cupped his face with both hands. He opened his eyes just in time to see Julie peer at him intently.

He wondered what she saw. Was she scared by the darkness in his eyes? She should be. She should be running far away. Didn't she know that he could pounce at any moment?

"Do you hurt anywhere?"

"Hurt?" he repeated. She had a tender expression that twisted him up inside.

"Any aching?"

Oh, hell, yeah. He was beginning to ache. Eric shifted in his seat. "Were you a nurse in a former life?"

There was a mysterious, almost bittersweet smile. "At one time I thought about it, but I decided I don't like hanging around hospitals."

"I know the feeling." When he was on enforced bed rest from his knife injury he almost went stir-crazy.

"I saw how nicely the doctors sewed you up." She reached out and brushed her fingertips along the side of his ribs.

He remembered how he'd woken up that morning. Half-naked with Julie, soft and warm underneath him. She had fit snugly against him. The memory made him rock hard.

"You probably haven't fully recovered." She continued to caress his scar, almost absently. "You should rest more."

He scowled at her suggestion. "I've been resting for the past six weeks."

"No, you haven't," she disagreed softly. "You've been working night and day to help Perry. I admire that about you. Not many guys would take the time to help their godfathers."

"It's the least I could do." He was uncomfortable by the admiring gleam in her eyes. He wasn't a hero because he was helping a friend. "Perry took care of me plenty of times when I was growing up."

"I bet you were wild." Her eyes sparkled.

"I was." Had she moved closer or had he? It didn't matter. He needed to break the spell between them.

She arched one eyebrow. "Are you still wild?"

His chest tightened. "Yeah," he confessed.

"Good," she whispered. "I like wild."

JULIE'S HEART POUNDED against her chest as she grazed her mouth against his. She thought she would feel brazen at this moment. Instead, she was nervous, not knowing if Eric was going to reject her.

She placed her hands on his shoulders and deepened the kiss. He tasted good. Hot, male and dangerous.

Eric didn't respond. She wanted one more taste before he pulled away. With the dart of her tongue, Julie traced the lines of his mouth, encouraging him to part his lips.

She heard Eric groan, felt the rumble in his chest. He reached out and Julie was sure he would push her away. Instead, he grabbed her waist, his hands bunching her dress in his fists.

Julie wasn't sure why he wasn't tumbling her into his arms or, worse, setting her aside. When she felt the tremor in his shoulders, she understood. He was trying to hang on to the last shred of restraint.

She understood it because she felt the same way. But she wasn't going to hold back any longer.

Julie thrust her tongue into Eric's warm mouth and boldly explored. When Eric sucked her in deep, Julie moaned with pleasure.

The sound of her voice shattered the last of his resistance. He vaulted from his chair and pressed her body against his. Eric speared his hands through her hair, holding her still before he plunged his tongue into her mouth.

His kiss made her knees buckle. She had never been kissed like this before. He dominated. Mastered. Claimed. She surrendered without a fight.

Julie grabbed the front of Eric's shirt and pulled him down with her. She lay across his desk, disregarding the pile of papers and whatever it was poking against her. All of her attention was on Eric.

She felt the urgency rippling through him as he rubbed his hands over her hips and stomach. His fierce kisses left her breathless. It was all Julie could do to hang on, her senses going wild. She inhaled his heat, his scent, and found it intriguing.

Eric was hot for her. He wanted her as much as she wanted him. She thought her seduction would end with a few kisses. She never thought it would go this far... that he wanted more. The knowledge filled her with confidence. She reached down to the tie at her waist and yanked it boldly. Her dress sagged open.

Eric broke the kiss and lifted his head. She pulled at her dress even more and watched his eyes darken with pleasure when he saw the pale blue lace of her bra.

He brushed her hands away and grabbed her dress. With his chest rising and falling with each ragged breath, he peeled her dress from her body. Julie's breath hitched in her throat. It felt as if he were unwrapping a special present.

A tingle of nerves washed over her. Did he like what he saw? Or was it going to end before it began? Julie was tempted to strike a centerfold pose to show her body off in the best light.

Eric covered one of her breasts with his strong hand. She felt small and soft against him. Ultrafeminine. He teased her tight nipple against the satin and she shivered with delight.

He leaned down, yanked the bra away and licked the tip of her breast. He curled his tongue, then flattened it, before sweeping it against her nipple. Heat washed through her as he teased her.

Julie cried out. She clutched his head, her fingers caressing his hair, as she pressed him closer. She wanted more.

As he sucked her nipple, Eric trailed his hand down her abdomen, stroking her heated skin, learning the curves of her body. She tensed when he cupped her sex.

Even though she still wore pale blue panties, there was no way she could hide her arousal. He touched her boldly, dragging the edge of his thumb along the folds of her sex. She wanted him to rip her panties off and sink into her.

The phone next to her head rang. The shrill sound made her jump. She looked around, startled, but Eric rested his hand against her shoulder to soothe her.

"Ignore it," he said against her breast, his voice low and rough. He slipped his fingertips beneath the lace of her panties. She desperately wanted to pretend nothing else existed but Eric and her.

"It's an in-office ring." It rang again and then stopped. Panic fluttered inside her chest. "If you don't answer, someone will come looking for you."

"I won't answer the door," he promised and did something with his tongue that sent a spray of wild sensations down her spine.

"But I didn't lock it," she said between gasps.

"Why would you? You didn't know…" Tension flooded his body. She knew the moment he'd figured out her plans. Eric pulled his hands away and raised his head. His eyes were an intense blue and he glared accusingly at her. "You set me up."

Her first instinct was to apologize, but she bit back the words. She didn't have anything to feel sorry about. "I didn't think it would go this far, Eric." She could tell by the look in his eyes that he didn't believe her. "But a deal's a deal," she said, her voice quavering. "I get to be a decoy."

4

ERIC TOOK A STEP BACK and Julie used the opportunity to scurry off his desk. "I can't believe it," he muttered dazedly.

She wondered what he meant as she quickly fastened her bra, not looking at him. What couldn't he believe? She thought as she hastily tied her dress with fumbling fingers. That she had seduced him?

Yeah, she couldn't believe it, either.

Eric sat down in his chair, his legs sprawled out as if they couldn't support him. His shirt was creased, his short hair mussed and his mouth was reddened by kisses.

He was the sexiest man she'd ever seen. Julie wished she could straddle his legs, rip open the wrinkled shirt and go wild on him.

Eric splayed his arms out. "What the hell?" he asked.

The straddling was obviously going to have to wait. Her skin may still be tingling, but Eric wouldn't touch her with a ten-foot pole.

Julie glanced away, unwilling for him to see the lust

shining in her eyes. She belatedly noticed that the sash of her dress was a mess and hurriedly untied it.

She didn't mean to flash him. She really didn't.

Eric hissed air between his clenched teeth. "Julie."

"Sorry," she muttered and tied her sash in a tangled knot before smoothing her hair with her hands. She knew she was a wreck. Like she'd just rolled around the desk with a hot, gorgeous guy. A guy who was still staring at her as if she were a threat.

No one had ever looked her at like that before. She usually went unnoticed and hated it, but this was uncomfortable. Unsettling. She wasn't sure if she liked it.

Eric leaned forward, his elbows on his knees, as he pinned her with an intense glare. "How far did you plan for it to go?"

Her face heated. If she told him she had been aiming for a kiss, he'd think she was far too innocent for him. "It wasn't really a plan…."

"I should have known." A muscle bunched in his cheek. "Reckless as always."

"It was more of a—" she waved her hand in the air, her limbs felt uncoordinated and jittery "—vague idea."

"Vague idea," he repeated dully. Eric closed his eyes and shoved his hands in his hair. "I could have sworn you were with me every step of the way."

"I was," she answered hoarsely. "Several steps ahead of you, actually."

But Eric didn't seem to be listening as he shook his head slowly. "If the phone hadn't rung, I would be deep inside of you right now."

Julie's legs wobbled as she squeezed her eyes shut. She easily imagined Eric's long, powerful thrusts into her. Filling, stretching and driving deep. Julie shuddered and opened her eyes to find Eric right in front of her.

She jumped back in surprise and her legs hit the couch. She struggled to keep her balance as Eric towered over her. It was difficult to maintain a distance when she inhaled his scent.

"You shouldn't tease a man like that." His quiet tone was at odds with the fierce energy pulsing from him. "It's dangerous."

Julie didn't feel as if she had been in any danger. She felt as if a present had been ripped from her hands just when she had unwrapped it. Hopeful but dissatisfied.

Eric didn't look hopeful. He stood close but was careful not to touch her. As if a brush of skin, a simple touch, would crumble his restraint. One word, one look, and he was hers.

Julie's breath hitched in her throat when she recognized she held this kind of sexual power over Eric. She nervously licked her lips and Eric's hot gaze followed the movement.

"You're lucky I stopped when I did," he said, sounding raw.

"Funny—" she tried to drawl the word as her heart pumped ferociously "—I was just going to say the same to you."

Eric's eyes narrowed. He didn't like that, she noted with a spurt of pleasure. He didn't like how she could wield this power over him, and he absolutely didn't like that she knew it, too.

If only she knew why she had him under her spell and how she could use this power. For good, of course.

Okay, maybe for evil, too. She didn't want to be the good girl of his dreams. She wanted to be the bad girl of his deepest, dirtiest fantasies.

She swayed toward him just as she heard a cursory knock on the door. Julie's heart leaped and Eric stepped away. She watched like a deer caught in the headlights as the door swung open.

"Eric?" Perry Gunthrie stepped into the office. "Oh, I didn't know you were here, Julie. Sorry to interrupt, but Eric, do you have a moment?"

The sight of her boss was like a splash of cold water. She was torn with the need to get him out of the room and the need to tell him about her new assignment. As much as she disliked the intrusion, she knew that timing was crucial. If she wanted to become a decoy, she had to work fast before Eric backed out on the deal.

"Perry, guess what?" she asked as she walked over to him. She caught a glimpse of Eric as he returned to his desk. He was on full alert, ready to pounce at any sign of trouble. "You can be the first to congratulate me."

"What for, Julie?" Perry asked indulgently.

Julie linked her arm with Perry's and looked directly at Eric. "Eric agreed that I can be the decoy."

Eric didn't say anything. He remained still and there was no change in his expression, but Julie felt the darkening of his mood. Julie tensed, wondering if he was going to renege on the deal.

"Really?" Perry's gravelly voice rose in surprise. "That's wonderful, honey." He patted her hand that rested on his arm and focused on his godson. "What changed your mind, Eric?"

Julie's gaze sharpened on Eric, but he kept his attention on the older man.

"Julie can be very persuasive."

She didn't like his tone, but she was thankful Eric wasn't any more forthcoming. She wasn't ashamed of their deal. It had been an impetuous bet, but it had worked in her favor.

She would not feel guilty about this. She gave him fair warning. She didn't pretend or fake her responses.

"Julie's enthusiasm is contagious," Perry admitted.

"I don't know about that," Eric said with a shrug. "But she'll do anything to get her man."

"I am in the room, you guys," Julie reminded them, casting a warning glare at Eric.

"Are you sure about this?" Perry asked Eric.

Julie's heart stopped when he hesitated for a brief moment. "Yes," he replied with great reluctance. "A deal is a deal."

Her heart beat double time. Julie pressed her lips together to prevent the squeal of delight. She was going to be a decoy!

"But don't worry, Perry," he said with a smile that didn't reach his eyes. "I will watch over her every step of the way. She won't make a move without my permission."

"What?" The thrill she felt vanished like a puff of smoke. Julie pulled her hand away from Perry. "What are you talking about?"

"Julie has the job, but she has no training," Eric continued as if she hadn't interrupted. "This position has a probation period. If she can't do the job, we'll find another decoy."

Of all the nerve! Julie placed her hands on her hips. "That wasn't agreed on. I'm perfectly capable of handling this assignment without a babysitter."

Eric crossed his arms. "I disagree."

Perry cleared his throat with an uncomfortable cough. "Perhaps I should leave you two to agree on the details," he said as he inched out of the room. "Eric, come to my office when you're finished."

Julie didn't say a word as she listened to Perry whistling the *Murder, She Wrote* theme song as he walked down the hall. She was very aware that the office door was wide open. She knew the people in the nearby cubicles were trying to listen in as they pretended to work. She was tempted to slam the door shut, but that would create more interest in her colleagues.

"You have no right to change our agreement," she whispered fiercely.

"I have every right," he said as he straightened his desk.

"Why am I the only one on probation?" She briefly looked over her shoulder before lowering her voice. "Is this because you lost a bet?"

He shook his head as if he couldn't believe she would question his decision. "Everything about the premarital screening is dependent on the decoy. If you can't entrap our target, we need to find someone who can."

"I seduced you," she pointed out. "Is that proof enough that I can be a decoy?" Julie cringed, wishing she hadn't said those words.

He shot a cautionary glance.

"What more do you want?" she asked as exasperation bled into her voice. "Another demonstration?"

Oh, crap. She couldn't believe she said that. Actually, she could. She wanted to demonstrate how she felt. She wanted another chance to roll around his desk. Her skin was still flushed, her veins buzzing with excitement and the longing inside her was a low, insistent ache.

She watched with a mix of trepidation and exhilaration as Eric rounded the desk. She saw the guarded expression in his eyes and disappointment crashed inside her. He wasn't going to let her get close to him again.

"This conversation is over. I need to meet with Perry."

She followed him out of his office. "I know that you're angry because you lost the deal. But that doesn't give you the right to make me suffer. You never struck me as petty."

Eric turned and she had to stop abruptly or risk plowing into his lean, muscular chest. She looked up into his stormy blue eyes.

"Don't you get it?" he asked. "You are my responsibility. Your safety is my top priority. I know it's not yours."

She shrugged at the idea. "It is."

"I predict that on your first assignment you will throw yourself headfirst into danger to succeed. I'm not going to tolerate that."

He was correct in assuming she would do anything to succeed, but she would take calculated risks. "I don't need to be protected. I am going to be an equal member of this team."

"That position needs to be earned." The look in his eye indicated she had a long way to go. "A team member, a partner, has to prove to be reliable and trust-worthy."

She had all those qualities. Every boring, unglamor-ous one of them. "Ask anyone in this office and they'll tell you how dependable I am."

"I don't need to ask anyone. Right now I don't trust you."

That hurt, but she knew why he felt that way. "I understand that." She raised her hands in surrender. "The bet was a bad idea, but I want you to know that I wouldn't have made it with just anyone."

"Doesn't matter. Today the only thing you proved to me is that you're not the woman I thought you were."

Julie's mouth fell open as she watched Eric leave and walk to Perry's office. What did that mean? That she wasn't a Goody Two-shoes? That the girl next door was just as dangerous to his senses as the femme fatale he met in exotic cities?

What it really meant was that she messed up. Big-time. She leaned against the wall and sighed. Sure, she got the assignment but she lost the chance to have something special with Eric.

ERIC WAS DETERMINED TO spend the next day in his of-fice. He needed to clear his head and stay away from Julie. He didn't want to look at her, hear her laugh or inhale her perfume.

Though it didn't take long for him to acknowledge that barricading himself in his office wasn't going to work.

He heard her familiar footsteps in the hallway. As much as he tried to ignore everything around him, he now knew that Julie walked by his office at least twice an hour.

And that his gut clenched in anticipation every time he heard her footsteps.

Eric stared at his computer screen with more focus than necessary. The door was closed, but he refused to look in that direction as Julie strode back to her cubicle. He needed to stay away, for his sake as well as hers.

The way he had felt yesterday was untamed, almost primal. One taste of Julie and he was ready to take her on his desk and mate like an animal.

He rubbed his face with his hands and stared at the screen. He had no idea what he was looking at. It was difficult keeping his mind on work when all he could think about was Julie, lying on his desk, baring herself to him.

What was she wearing underneath her clothes today?

Eric grunted with self-disgust and stood up. He couldn't take it anymore. The image of Julie, a tantalizing mix of innocence and sensuality, was too much for him. He had to leave his office, but as soon as he stepped outside, he would see her. Be drawn to her. Fantasize about her.

Eric took a deep breath. If he could get through the most high-tech security and sneak past enemy lines, he could manage a simple coffee run without looking at a specific cubicle. He didn't know why Julie Kent rattled his senses, but he wasn't going to let it continue.

He opened his office door and kept his head down as he crossed the threshold. Eric only took a few steps before he automatically looked at Julie's work space.

Eric slowed his pace as he stared. Julie was standing

as she stacked a pile of uniforms. She wore a yellow sleeveless dress that skimmed her curves. Her brown hair fell in waves against her shoulders. Her lips were pink and kissable. There wasn't anything suggestive about her appearance, but he couldn't stop looking. Julie appeared soft and feminine.

Julie flipped her hair off her shoulders and their gazes connected. He felt the energy crackling between them before her eyelashes fluttered down.

"Eric!" Martha greeted him excitedly, effectively cornering him. "I have the perfect mark for our test run."

"Uh…okay." Eric dragged his gaze away from Julie and bent his head so he could meet Martha's eyes. "Please tell me it's not your husband."

Martha laughed and gave a light slap on his arm. "No, no, no. That wouldn't be any fun."

"Good." He felt Julie's gaze on him. He glanced back but she was looking away. Strange. He usually could tell if he were being watched.

"It's Lloyd." She looked at him expectantly and clucked her tongue when Eric shrugged. "I know I must have mentioned him. Lloyd is my daughter's boyfriend."

Eric winced. That's almost as bad as volunteering the husband. "That could get messy."

"Not at all. My daughter knows nothing about this."

"Even messier." Martha was good at solving puzzles and scary smart when it came to math, but unlike her detective hero Miss Marple, the way people acted was a mystery to Martha.

"I know that Lloyd is a good guy, but is he good for

my daughter?" Martha leaned in closer and whispered conspiratorially, "She once dated a serial cheater and I don't think she could cope with that again. I just want to see what Lloyd is like when he's faced with temptation."

They needed a target for a trial run and Eric would prefer someone who wasn't dangerous, psychotic or a sleazebag. "Are you sure you want do this? What if he takes the bait?"

"I doubt he will."

Martha didn't seem particularly worried, but people have a tendency to surprise. After all, he had been wrong about Julie.

He felt the irresistible lure of Julie and glanced in her direction. She looked up and met his gaze boldly.

Eric broke eye contact. He was usually good about sizing people up. After being out in the field for so long, an agent honed that intuition. But Julie's action had blindsided him. Either his razor-sharp instincts were blurring or he saw what he wanted to see in Julie. The woman of his dreams and fantasies didn't really exist.

But the woman who had lain on his desk was an intriguing puzzle. That Julie wasn't someone he had to approach with caution. That Julie wouldn't break at the first sign of trouble or make a run for it when he didn't feel so gentlemanly.

Which was most of the time when he was around her.

"Here's a picture of Lloyd." Martha pulled up a photo on her cell phone and handed it to him.

The guy was a geek. Eric studied the picture of the spiky hair, pale skin kid. The red T-shirt overwhelmed Lloyd's lanky physique.

"What does he do for a living?" Eric asked as he seriously considered Martha's idea. The guy had a goofy smile and there was an openness about him.

"He's a computer programmer for a video game company. Z-Tron or Z-Ray. Something that has to do with zombies."

A computer geek who spent most of his time on video games. Perfect. If Lloyd made a move on Julie, she could snap him like a twig.

"Okay, we'll do it," Eric decided as he handed the phone back to Martha. "I'll inform Perry and we'll start the process."

"I can't wait!"

Eric wished he could share that feeling. He looked in Julie's direction just as her gaze darted away.

Martha saw what caught his attention. "Julie is going to make a great decoy."

"I hope so." As much as he disliked the idea of Julie being the decoy, he didn't want to throw her into a baptism of fire.

Martha bumped her elbow against his arm. "What do you think of the alias she's trying out?" she whispered.

Eric frowned. "Alias?"

"Asia calls it Siren Julie."

Siren. Wasn't that a female mythological creature who lured sailors to their death by her singing? Only Julie wasn't using her voice. "And the eyes?"

"Oh, you caught that." She patted his arm. "Good for you, but she's still practicing."

He didn't like the sound of that. "Practicing what?"

"Julie's luring unsuspecting men with her eyes. I taught her that this morning."

Eric glanced down at the older woman with surprise. "You did?"

"Of course," Martha said with an exaggerated flutter of her eyelashes before she strutted away. "It's how I met my husband."

Eric stared coldly at Julie. She was practicing on him again. Did she think he was made of steel? That he wouldn't take what she was pretending to offer? This woman needed to understand that there were consequences to her actions.

He marched over to her cubicle. Julie showed no concern or trepidation. Instead, she looked at him from under her lashes and a slow, triumphant smile tugged at her lips. As if her eye technique worked.

Which it did. Damn it.

Julie flipped her hair back. "What can I do for you, Eric?" she asked softly.

He curled his hands on the edge of her cubicle wall. "You do not want to practice on me."

"Why?" She leaned back in her chair. "Are you in danger of taking up my offer?"

"Stop that." He dug his fingers into the edge.

Her eyes seemed to grow impossibly big. "Stop what?"

"Siren Julie. I know all about the alias."

She tilted her head. "And you don't like it?"

"No." He liked her soft femininity, but he didn't like her practicing her flirting techniques on him.

"I'm just trying to prove that I can be smart and sexy," she said as a blush stained her cheeks. "Two qualities you seem to think I'm lacking."

If she knew how sexy he thought she was, there

would be no stopping her. "I also mentioned cautious. Why don't you work on that first?"

"Caution is overrated. Anyway, I like it wild," she said shyly.

She'd said something similar yesterday right before she kissed him. "This is your last warning, Julie. Stop practicing your seduction techniques on me. In fact, don't practice it on any guy in this office."

Julie's mouth fell open and her coy attitude disappeared. "Do you really think I would use these techniques on Max? Or Perry?"

"Please." He held up his hand to stop her. "I could do without that visual."

She slowly rose from her seat. "Eric, you have nothing to worry about. The only man I'm practicing on is you."

Eric wanted to roll his eyes at that statement. "Sure you are."

"I promise."

"And how did I get to be the lucky one?"

"Simple." She leaned over her desk and gripped the cubicle wall, her hands next to his. "You're the safest one to try on."

He pulled his hands away as if he'd been burned. "Are you kidding me?" He was a beast compared to the men in Julie's life. He would break her heart no matter how careful he would be.

"You said so yourself," Julie said. "There's no way anything can happen between us. First of all, you don't trust my motivations."

"That's true."

Her gaze slid away. "You've also made it very clear

that I couldn't possibly compete with the trained se-ductresses of your past."

"And yet you wind up on my desk half-naked."

"Which I didn't mind at all," she said matter-of-factly, "but I know it's due to lack of sleep and your slow recovery."

"Now you're making excuses for me?" He leaned in, doing his best to ignore her delicious scent, and waited until she looked back at him. "Have you considered that I am not a nice guy? That I'm actually the kind of man your mother warned you about?"

Julie's eyelashes flickered as if the thought hadn't occurred to her. "Not possible. You would never take advantage of a good girl like me."

He stared into her eyes. Was she playing him? Or was she really that innocent?

She winked.

He wanted to growl. Give her a taste of the dark sexual need swirling inside him. Instead, he pushed away from the cubicle wall and strode off. "Don't test your luck with me or you will find out just what kind of man I really am."

Her husky laugh followed him. "I'm looking forward to it."

5

SEVERAL DAYS LATER, Eric was bracing himself before he left his desk. He shook his head in wonder. Two months ago—hell, two weeks ago—he wouldn't have considered Gunthrie S&I a hazardous workplace. He had dealt with violent criminals, pathological liars and burned-out colleagues in his D.C. office. None of that prepared him for Julie and her sexy aliases just outside his door.

Each day had been a different look. It was as if she hadn't gotten enough chances to play dress-up as a child. But there was nothing innocent about these disguises. Each alias was an onslaught to his senses.

Tuesday had been a tough day when she showed up as Glamorous Julie. She had paid attention to detail and the result was breathtaking. Julie had worn her hair up in a tight twist and he had been itching to rip out the pins and let her hair fall. She had worn a pale pink dress with a deep neckline. Her simple diamond necklace had been strategically placed to drag the eye to her cleavage. He hadn't been able to stop staring at her breasts and remembering how perfect they felt in his hands.

Bad Girl Julie on Wednesday had been worse. She had owned that look, Eric reluctantly admitted. Julie had brimmed with attitude when she wore skintight jeans and a black bra that peeked out from under her white tank top. He had enjoyed how she had strutted in her knee-high black boots. Eric had been tempted too many times to pull at her ponytail, wrap it around his hand and then tame her with one hot kiss.

He barely got through Wednesday and then Thursday happened. Trashy Julie, she had explained to the group of men who had suddenly gravitated to her cubicle. Eric never thought she could have pulled off that alias. But she had, with the heavy makeup and naturally sensuous movements.

Her brown hair had been wild and sexy, but it hadn't been able to compete with her red cotton top that was more corset than camisole. Yet it had been the Daisy Duke shorts that sent his blood pressure soaring. Her hips had been barely concealed in the faded shorts and she had swayed provocatively when she walked in her red platform heels. When he had caught a glimpse of the henna tramp stamp, he hadn't trusted the lock on his door or his rapidly declining self-control. He had to leave the office.

Now that he thought about it, the sexiness of the aliases had been escalating. Eric rubbed his hand over his face and took a deep breath. He didn't know what to expect, especially since it was Casual Friday. Bikini Julie?

He refused to speculate anymore. Julie's role-playing was getting more brazen at the same rate his restraint was weakening. But he had to see her or he'd imagine all kinds of aliases throughout the day. Once he saw her, he had to keep his distance and not make contact.

He wanted to get this over quickly. Eric wrenched open the door, stepped across the threshold and glanced in Julie's direction. He froze as his gut squeezed hard.

Almost Bare Julie. The label wafted through his sluggish brain. That's what he would call it.

He slowly blinked, unable to tear his gaze away from her. Julie wore a flirty, loose, one-shoulder dress. It kind of reminded him of a toga. A short, navy-blue toga that exposed a lot of bare leg. Her shoes were delicate strappy things. If he chased her, she wouldn't get far.

Damn. Why did have to think about that? He should have locked himself in the office.

What was it about the dress? His gaze focused sharply on Julie as his body hardened. It didn't accentuate her figure, but it looked as if it could fall off at any minute. It made him think of rumpled sheets. Like she just got out of bed and gathered a sheet around her. One sharp pull and the dress would fall.

Julie tilted her head back and laughed, her hair cascading down in waves. Eric shifted his attention to the man at her side. His shaven head and muscular build indicated that he was one of the security guards on the payroll.

Eric caught the man's salacious grin and wanted to knock it off his face. He glared at the man, noticing his macho stance and the puffed-up chest.

He couldn't tell if Julie noticed it, too. She was chatting away as she handed the man a folded uniform.

The man rested his hand against the wall behind Julie and leaned in. He was about to make a move on her.

Eric made a step to intervene but stopped when he watched Julie laugh and blush. She said something he couldn't catch but it made the security guard smile. She patted the guy's muscular arm and smoothly side-stepped his maneuver.

Interesting. Eric watched Julie walk away from the security guard with a friendly wave. He was surprised that she didn't get flustered. That she handled the guy with aplomb.

But then, Julie could twist *him* into knots without any effort. Eric's breath lodged in his chest as he stared at her long, bare legs. Julie walked with confidence, as if she knew she had everyone's attention.

And she was now walking toward him. He flexed his hands as he struggled to remain still. If she knew he couldn't stop looking at her, that he was powerless to her feminine charms, nothing would stop her.

Eric kept his stony expression as desire licked through his veins. She graced him with a sunny smile and strode past him.

He was at her side before he even realized it.

"Was that guy bothering you?" he asked, looking over his shoulder and glaring at the security guard who was still watching her ass.

"Who, Snake? No, not at all."

"Snake?" Eric raised an eyebrow in disbelief. "The guy's name is Snake?"

"It's a nickname because of his tattoo."

"Sure it is," he muttered. "I didn't see a tattoo."

"He just offered to show it to me, but I declined."

Eric placed a proprietary hand on Julie's back. He

knew he shouldn't feel territorial. Julie was not his, but he didn't want any other guy where he couldn't go.

"Anyway, he didn't recognize me in this alias," she said with a chuckle. "He asked what happened to the old uniform girl."

"The outfits you're wearing are not appropriate." Great. Now he sounded like an old, conservative man.

"I know," Julie said with a nod, surprising him. "Perry understands that we are crunched for time and I'm using office hours to try on different aliases. He doesn't mind."

I mind. "I meant it wasn't appropriate for decoying."

That made her stop. She looked at Eric as if he'd said something crazy, and glanced down at her dress. "I disagree. It's perfect."

The dress was perfect for Julie. As if it had been made especially for her. She exuded an innate sensuality that made heads turn. "Think of it from a security point of view," he suggested. "How are you going to protect yourself? Your hair can be used against you."

She rolled her eyes. "You also said that when I had my hair back in a ponytail. I'm not cutting my hair."

Good. He didn't want that, either. He liked the feel of her hair in his hands. Enjoyed tangling it between his fingers. "And your legs are completely bare," he added gruffly.

"That's the idea."

"You should wear jeans for protection." His eyes drifted to her light pink toenails. Her feet looked soft and delicate. "And I forbid you to wear those shoes."

"Forbid?" She drew the word out, shook her head and started walking.

He was right at her side. "If you have to defend your-self, you can't use them as a weapon. Kick a guy and you'll break your toes."

"Eric," she said with a long-suffering sigh. "When I put together this alias, I wasn't thinking about defensive maneuvers. I was thinking about sex."

His entire body clenched. "So is everyone else," he said through gritted teeth.

"Like I said, the dress is perfect."

"I would say reckless." Which was why it suited Julie so well. "You're not taking the potential threats seriously."

"Oh, I think you're taking it seriously enough for the both of us."

ERIC CIRCLED HIS HAND around her upper arm and pulled her out of the hallway. He quickly escorted her through a doorway into a dark room.

Julie felt the door close behind her. She inhaled the scent of paper and knew she was in the supply closet before he flipped on the light switch. The light revealed a cramped storage room filled with shelves and boxes.

Julie leaned against the closed door. She wanted to appear nonchalant, but if Eric looked closely, he would see the pulse point at the base of her neck was jumping wildly. She had longed to be alone with him, but Eric had kept a safe distance.

Until now. And she wasn't going to waste this opportunity.

"Is this going to be another self-defense class?" she asked, adding in a small yawn and stretch.

"You need it." He placed his hands on the door, effectively trapping her.

Did he realize what he was doing? She bit her lip to prevent a smile. Didn't he know that she had no urge to escape?

"You can't rely solely on your colleagues," he said. "I just pulled you aside and no one noticed."

"Don't worry about them." She tilted her head up and her face was close to his, almost touching. "They'll watch like hawks when I'm a decoy."

"Don't be too sure about that," he said quietly.

Julie held his gaze. "And you wouldn't let anything happen to me," she said softly.

"Things go wrong," he insisted, his voice low and gritty. "What if your target figures out he's being set up? He corners you. What do you do?"

She wasn't going to wait for him to make the next move. It was time to stop fantasizing and go for it. She curled her arms over Eric's strong shoulders and linked her hands behind his head. "I cling against him and move him closer."

She saw the desire. "Julie…"

"Eric…"

He reached for her hands and raised them above her head. The position placed her at a disadvantage, but it also brought Eric closer.

"What if I pin you to the door?" he asked roughly. "You're powerless."

"Not quite." She felt alive. Sensual. Slightly out-of-control. Julie arched her spine and pressed her breasts against his hard chest before rocking her hips against him.

His fingers squeezed against her wrists. The telltale movement excited her. "Defenseless," he said roughly as he leaned into her.

She lifted her foot out of her sandal and grazed her foot against his leg.

Eric squeezed his eyes shut. She knew he was at the breaking point.

"Julie, I warned you about trying these aliases on me. Stop it now or there will be consequences."

Julie flicked her tongue along his mouth. Her breath hitched in her throat when she saw the hungry gleam in his eyes. Dark excitement curled in the pit of her stomach.

Eric's mouth came down on hers. It was a clash of lips, teeth and tongues. It was aggression and pure need. This was what she longed for, Julie thought wildly as desire coiled low in her pelvis. She didn't want Eric to treat her as a princess. She wanted him to treat her like a woman.

Eric let go of her wrists and she took immediate advantage of her release by grabbing his shirt. She yanked it out of his pants, pulling at his buttons with wild abandon as she kissed him hungrily.

She pushed his shirt past his shoulders, her movements hurried and desperate. She needed to see him and feel his muscles clench under her touch. She wanted to taste his hot skin and listen to him moan.

Julie felt his big, masculine hand on her shoulder. She felt him push down her shoulder strap. One fierce tug and her dress slid to her waist, pooling at her hips. Her breasts were naked, her nipples tight with anticipation.

Eric's forceful kisses bruised her mouth and he claimed her breasts with his hands. His skin was rough against her flesh, the friction heightening her arousal. Julie groaned and pulled him closer. She wanted his hands all over her.

He tore his mouth from her lips, his breath harsh and uneven to her ears. Eric rested his forehead against hers and she felt him trying to hold back and gather the last of his self-control. That was the last thing she wanted. She needed his mouth on her breasts. She wanted him to lick her. Bite. Tease. She pushed at his shoulders.

Eric bent down and captured her nipple with his mouth. She shivered with delight. Julie closed her eyes as he teased her with his tongue and the sharp edge of his teeth. Her skin felt tight and tingly. He drew her nipple in his mouth and she felt the pull all the way to her core.

Eric grabbed her dress from her waist and pulled it past her hips. She only wore a pair of black lace panties. The fragile lace felt heavy and constricting. She had to get them off right now.

Julie hooked her thumbs in the waistband and shucked them off. She stepped out of them and impatiently kicked her clothes to the side. She stood before him only in a pair of shoes as Eric cupped her.

Julie spread her legs wide as he stroked the folds of her sex. She rocked her head from side to side as he dipped one finger, then two, inside her. When he teased her clit with his thumb, her mind slowly shut down.

He pressed down hard and lust blazed through her as the all-consuming pleasure overtook her. Eric covered his mouth with hers before she let out a cry.

The sensations were still rippling through her when Eric grabbed her hips and turned her around. The sudden move was disorienting and Julie automatically flattened her palms on the wood door to maintain her balance.

This wasn't what she had planned. She wanted to wrap her legs around Eric's lean waist and hold on tight as he drove deep in her. This way she had no control over him. The loss of power was as startling as it was thrilling.

Her heart pounded against her chest when she heard the rustle of his jeans and the metallic sound of his zipper. Eric seized her hips again. Placing his leg between hers, she spread her feet so she had a wider stance, offering a naughty, sinful invitation.

Julie trembled when she felt the rounded tip of his thick cock pressing against her flesh. When Eric filled her completely, a low guttural groan escaped her throat.

She laid her head against the door as the conflicting, incredible sensations overpowered her. She closed her eyes, inhaling Eric's aroused scent as he placed his hands over hers, reassuring her.

Julie rocked her hips against him, urging him to unleash his strength and power. She wanted to experience his unbridled passion.

Eric gave a warning growl and reached under her arms to squeeze her breasts. She arched her spine, thrusting her breasts farther into his hands, enjoying how the sting heightened her pleasure.

Julie bit her lip as her desire intensified. Eric might think he was in the dominant position, but she wasn't going to yield to his every command. She clenched her inner muscles, smiling wickedly when she heard his sharp intake of breath. She loved the tremor in his fingers as he trailed his hand down her stomach.

Her smile slipped when Eric captured her swollen clit. A groan escaped her throat as he teased her nipple and clit as he gave a shallow thrust.

"More," she pleaded.

He let go of her breast and dragged the heavy curtain of her hair over her shoulder to expose her neck.

"Are you sure?" Eric asked, his warm breath wafting over her sweat-slickened skin.

"Please." She hated how quickly she surrendered, but she was desperate for the satisfaction that only Eric could give. No one had made her feel like this and no one ever would. "Please, Eric."

He pinched her nipple in response. She was very close to climaxing.

His hands clenched her hips, his fingers pressing into her skin, as he slowly withdrew. Julie's whimper dissolved in her chest as he drove his cock deep in her core. She rolled her hips again, silently encouraging him.

Eric pumped into her, slowly building momentum. Her legs shook and her hands slipped down the door as she met each thrust with the rock of her hips. Her heart raced, her throat ached with every breath, but her body was greedy. She was insatiable.

She capitulated to his primal rhythm as the white-hot pleasure rushed through her body. Julie sagged against the door as Eric pressed his face into her neck and muffled his cry of release.

Julie rested against the cool wood, breathing heavily as her body pulsated. She was still, but she felt different. Strong and beautiful.

So, this was what she had been missing. She had longed for this quick, wild coupling, but no man understood her desire. No man but Eric.

She felt his sigh of regret. "Crap," he muttered before he pulled away.

Julie winced. That wasn't very flattering. She had hoped they could do it again and again and again. He may have rocked her world, but Eric wasn't interested in repeating the experience.

"That's not what any woman wants to hear right after sex," Julie said in a brittle voice. She took a deep breath, put on a brave face and turned around. Her heart gave a funny flip at the sight of Eric. He was disheveled, half-naked and gloriously male.

He shoved his fingers in his hair. Something close to horror flickered in his eyes. "That shouldn't have happened."

Oh, great. It was going to be one of *those* postcoital talks. She should have known. She didn't want to hear it. Julie searched for her dress and quickly picked it up. "Well, it did and I don't regret it for one moment."

"How can you say that?" His gaze focused on the swell of her hips. His eyes darkened as he hissed with regret. "I should have stopped and…I want to apologize."

"I don't want to hear an apology. If I had wanted to stop, I would have said so." She tossed her dress over her head and slid it down her body, which still ached for his touch. Her movements were awkward and slow, but she had to get the hell out of here before he said anything else.

"We had unprotected sex." He shook his head at his lapse of judgment. "I would never intentionally put you at risk."

"It's okay." She bent down, snatched her panties and balled them up in her hands. She wanted to make a run for it and find a place where she could regain her composure. "I'm healthy and I'm on the Pill. I'm fully capable of protecting myself from an unexpected pregnancy."

"Julie...I—"

"If I didn't want this, I wouldn't have allowed you to touch me." She opened the door. "If it makes you feel any better, let's not talk about this ever again." She stepped out of the supply room and shut the door before he could say another word.

6

"I AM FINALLY DOING THIS!" Julie tried to contain her smile as she walked on the sky bridge that led to a popular nightclub in the center of Bellevue. A small group of women walked past her, a blur of chatter and perfume. She glanced out the window but the restaurants, spas and luxury boutiques were also a blur. The window displays and street lights were smears of color in the night. She barely saw the BMWs and Porsches competing for space on the busy street below her. All she heard was the beat of her heart mingling with the clacking of her heels on the cement. "Watch out, world, here I come!"

"Stay focused." Asia's voice was faint in the earpiece Julie wore.

"I'm sorry, but I can't contain my enthusiasm," Julie replied, noticing yet another handsome man in a designer suit leaning against a wall, obviously waiting for someone. He glanced up from his cell phone and checked her out. "I'm finally a Charlie's Angel."

"But better-dressed. Now stop talking to yourself or people will start staring."

"Ah, that would explain it." The man's attention returned to his phone. "I thought I was turning heads because of my general awesomeness."

"Let's transfer that awesomeness into the role."

"Done." She was going to act as if she were meant for the spotlight. She had no clue how to navigate a nightclub like this, but she wasn't going to let that stop her. She wasn't going to pause or hesitate. No nervously biting her lip or hugging the wall.

The nightclub was trendy, which she kind of expected since it was in the epicenter of Bellevue. The rich, the powerful and the spoiled lived around here. They were easily bored and difficult to please. She could act like that.

She approached the double door and frowned when she didn't recognize the music that pulsed through the walls. That was a problem. She had to acclimate herself to the culture and didn't know a very important part like music. What if she dressed all wrong? What if she didn't know which drink to buy?

Don't borrow trouble. Julie squared back her shoulders and strutted to the door, giving a short nod in the bouncer's direction.

"Wait." The bouncer held out his meaty hand and motioned for her to come closer. "Let's see some ID."

She was getting *carded?* She wasn't the type who went to nightclubs every week, but she was sure she looked over twenty-one. "Are you serious?" she asked.

He glared at her.

Apparently he was. She couldn't believe it. Julie

trudged over to where the bouncer stood. No Charlie's Angel had to deal with this type of humiliation.

Julie reached in her pocket, where she kept her cash and driver's license. She felt her face turn bright red as she presented the card to the bouncer.

"Don't you dare tell Eric," Julie muttered as Asia's laughter rang in her ear. She was thankful that Eric didn't witness this moment. She bet *he* didn't get carded.

The bouncer looked at the driver's license, then at her, then at the license again.

Oh, right. Julie grimaced. The photo on her license was nothing like what she was wearing. "I'm not photogenic."

The bouncer didn't disagree. After getting her ID back and her hand stamped, Julie walked into the nightclub. She paused at the entrance and looked around. It was bigger than she anticipated. Sleek and expensive.

"Oh, crap."

"What?" Asia asked urgently.

"This place isn't anything like the tequila bar where we hang out." She noticed the chrome-and-glass décor, the patrons in designer clothes and the large dance floor flickering with multicolored lights.

"Don't let it intimidate you," Asia said in a soothing voice, but the static ruined the effect.

She dressed all wrong, Julie decided as her stomach twisted with dread. She should have visited the place earlier. Tactical error on her part, but she had directed all her focus on her seduction techniques.

"What the hell are you wearing?"

Julie whirled around at the sound of Eric's voice. She didn't hear him approach. Her heart thudded against her rib cage as she stared at him, noting how good he looked in a black button-down shirt and dark jeans. She barely registered his stern expression. She remembered the hunger in his eyes, the way he was possessed when he'd claimed her.

She blinked and took a step back as desire tugged deep inside her. She wasn't going to get distracted. Not tonight. Not by Eric, who was waiting for her to mess up.

"And hello to you, too," Julie replied coolly.

"Is that Eric?" Asia's voice pierced into her ear. "Tell him I said hi."

Julie dipped her head. "Shut up, Asia. If I can't IM and email simultaneously, you know I can't do more than one conversation at a time."

"I'm serious, Julie," Eric said as he gave her clothes a critical appraisal. "What alias is this?"

"I call it Kick-Ass Julie." She wore her black leather boots, dark jeans, a tank top and a military-inspired olive-green jacket. It had seemed like a good idea at the time. Inspired, actually.

Eric looked at her as if she had lost her senses, but she would defend her decision to the end. His attention rested on her hair. "What did I tell you about the hair?" He glared at her high ponytail.

How could she explain that the style went with the outfit? "And here I thought you'd be thrilled that I'm completely covered." She pointed at her jacket with a flourish.

"I am," he said with a soft growl.

"Then why are you growling at me?"

"Because he's hot for you," Asia interjected.

Julie closed her eyes. "One more word from you, Asia, and I'm taking out the earpiece."

Eric's gaze swept down her body and her skin tingled. "Do you really think this is going to get your target in that outfit?"

She sighed. "Eric, do you know what Lloyd was wearing in that picture Martha provided?"

"A red T-shirt. What about it?"

"It was a T-shirt for a video game. It had a woman who has a long ponytail, a military jacket and long black boots."

Eric paused and she knew she'd surprised him by picking up on that detail. "That doesn't mean he's attracted to a video game character," he argued.

"Are you kidding? These video games allow guys to create their dream girls. They can choose what the heroine will look like, what they'll wear and how much they will jiggle." She motioned at her outfit. "His shirt had this girl on it and that's what I'm going with."

"Suit yourself."

"Thanks for the pep talk," she said dryly. "Which alias would you have recommended?"

His gaze grew intense for a second before he ruthlessly banked it. "Never mind."

"No, tell me."

He exhaled sharply. "It's too late to change, anyway."

She wanted to scream with frustration. Which alias did he think was the sexiest? No, he would never tell her. He would never give her that much power over him.

She'd find out on her own, but that was would have to wait. She slapped her hands together and rubbed her palms. "So, where's Lloyd?"

Eric looked past Julie's shoulder. "Our target is at the bar with two other friends."

She grimaced. It was going to be difficult separating him from the pack.

"Did Asia check the audio?" Eric asked.

"Triple-checked it," Asia chirped in Julie's ear. Julie simply nodded.

"Max is stationed near the bar and will take pictures with his digital camera. Try not to leave the bar."

"I will if he wants to dance." They had been through all this several times as they prepped for this night. She was ready for this. She felt like a fighter before leaving his corner. She wanted to move. She needed to get in there while her blood was pumping.

"I can't hear what's going on because some of our equipment just failed and there's no time to replace it." He clenched his jaw, the only physical sign of how he felt about that. She knew from their team meetings how much it bothered him that he wouldn't be in constant contact with her. "You remember the signal if you're in trouble."

"Yes." She wanted to bounce on her feet and throw a few punches. Anything to get rid of this excess energy.

"What's the signal?"

"Eric, don't crowd me," she pleaded as she took a couple of steps into the club. "Go away before you blow my cover."

He reached for her hand. It was firm but gentle. That surprised her. She looked into his eyes.

"Promise me that you'll back off if you get a bad vibe."

"I promise," she said and let go. She hated making that promise, but she did it for Eric's peace of mind.

Julie made her way to the bar and tried not to be obvious as she searched for her target. She noticed the women all wore very short, strapless dresses. Even the waitresses wore black camisoles and black short-shorts. She stuck out like a sore thumb. Her alias idea was going to be a disadvantage.

She found Lloyd at the bar just as Eric had said. Her eyes narrowed in on her target. He was tall and the spiky hair added a few inches. She suspected he wore baggy clothes to hide his skinny build.

Lloyd was leaning back on the bar stool, smiling as he listened to his friends try to impress two beautiful young women. It didn't look as if he was trying to win them over. Good. It meant she had a chance to swoop in and catch him.

Julie surveyed the area. She stalled when she glanced at the women with Lloyd's friends. A sense of uneasiness washed over her. Now she understood why Eric had a problem with her alias.

She took a closer look at the platinum blonde and voluptuous redhead who had taken command of the men's attention. Their beauty was exotic. They took sexy to a whole new level. Charlie's Angels wished they looked like these women.

There was no way she could compete with that. She saw how their skimpy dresses left little to the imagination. She figured these women were sexier than these guys had ever dreamed of.

It looked as if Blondie and Red were one step from being swept off to bed. They worked fast, but they didn't need to work hard to get a man's interest. Blondie was listening intently to Lloyd's shorter friend while Red had an arm draped on the other friend's shoulders.

Julie wanted to back away. Try again when she wasn't competing with that kind of in-your-face sexuality.

She took a step back and wavered. No, she couldn't back down. Not when everyone was watching. Waiting. She had to give it her best shot.

Julie jutted her chin out and strode to the empty seat next to Lloyd. If she gave up now, she'd never get another chance to play and would be permanently on the sidelines.

She wouldn't let that happen again.

Lloyd turned his head when she sat down. She smiled at him and rested her arms on the bar. The next few seconds were crucial and her heart was beating fast. If she blew this, they would get someone else to play decoy. This was her chance to show everyone she was smart and sexy. A woman of action. A woman who shouldn't be ignored.

She looked away to flag the bartender. Her hand trembled as the nervousness tumbled through her body. When she looked back, Lloyd was still looking at her.

Relief poured through her veins and her smile widened. Lloyd smiled back. The game was on.

WHY DIDN'T HE INSIST ON getting more audio equipment? Eric wondered as he leaned against a tall table next to the wall. The audio team texted him with updates, but it wasn't enough. He wanted to know every dirty thing Lloyd was saying to Julie.

Not that Julie seemed to mind. Eric wanted to growl. He took a sip of his water and wished it was something stronger. It appeared that Julie was enjoying herself. And why not? She was showing off, Eric thought as he glared over the glass rim, proving that she could be a decoy.

Giving in to temptation, Eric grabbed his cell phone and called Asia. She answered it on the third ring. "I'm working here, Eric."

"I want a status report," he said as he reined in his impatience.

"She's a great flirt," she said gleefully. "Who knew?"

He knew firsthand. It was uncomfortable watching Julie flirt with another man. Those brazen smiles and sly looks should be for him and he didn't like to share. When she had taken off her jacket, revealing a snug tank top, he wanted to go over and throw the jacket back onto her shoulders.

"Is she about to reel him in?"

"Give it time, Eric. The last thing she wants to do is spook him."

"I don't think I can take much more of this."

"Really? Because Julie looks like she could do it all night," Asia said with a throaty laugh before she disconnected the call.

Eric pocketed his phone and studied Julie. Asia was right. Julie was having the time of her life. There was a joy, an energy pouring out of her that no man could ignore. It was going to be impossible to keep her away from this.

And he didn't need Asia to tell him how well Julie was doing. Julie wasn't aggressive and showed great patience as she gradually lured Lloyd away from his friends. Julie knew how to use body language. She mirrored Lloyd's movements. When she wasn't touching her mouth, drawing attention to her lips, she was touching Lloyd.

The guy was no match for Julie. Lloyd was getting closer and closer. His hand rested on Julie's. His knees kept bumping against hers. When he leaned in to whisper something in Julie's ear, Eric wanted to jump from his seat, pull them apart and declare that Julie was his.

But that wasn't true. He'd had mind-blowing sex with Julie, but that didn't mean he had a claim on her. She didn't even want to talk about it afterward. Could he blame her? He took her against the door at the office. He took her like a hungry animal when she deserved something with a lot more sophistication.

She didn't want to talk about what happened because she saw the truth about him. He wasn't hero material. He wasn't the suave spy of her fantasies. He wasn't even a gentleman. That side of him no one—not even his parents—could love.

He had tried, but he couldn't hide his primitive nature. He didn't belong in Julie's world. She would never invite him into her bed or her home. He was meant to guard her ivory tower, not climb the wall and bed the princess.

Lloyd, with his porcupine hair and social awkwardness, was more of a prince than he'd ever be. Eric set his water glass down carefully. The guy didn't grab or tackle. He knew how to treat Julie right. Lloyd treated her as if she was a fantasy, a dream that could disappear if he moved too quickly.

Eric almost missed the tilt of Julie's head. His chest tightened. She was asking him if he wanted to go to her place. They had already come up with possible scenarios to extract her from actually having to go anywhere with a man. He knew this was important for their assignment, but his gut still twisted as he watched Julie invite another man to her home.

He watched Julie's face. He knew he should study the target's expression. Did her face soften like it had for him? Did her eyes sparkle? Would her expression be any different with another man?

His muscles locked and he was ready to pounce. The nightclub faded around him. The music drifted into a low buzz as he saw something like pain flicker in Julie's eyes.

Eric clenched his water glass. He didn't know what Lloyd said to Julie, but he would rip the giant geek apart. Eric saw Julie's smile tighten as she dipped her head in disappointment.

Lloyd glanced at his watch before he jumped off his bar stool. He gave an awkward wave before he walked over to his friends. Eric's gaze narrowed with confusion as he watched Lloyd slap his hand on his friend's back and say something before he headed for the exit.

Eric jerked his attention back to Julie. Her spine was straight and she looked away from where Lloyd's friends stood. She looked as if she didn't have a care in the world. Like all she wanted to do was finish her beer and soak up the atmosphere.

Eric knew it was all an act. Julie's confidence was shaken. Her first decoy assignment and the guy didn't take the bait.

He should feel relieved, but he felt her disappointment and knew it was tearing her up inside.

JULIE FELT ERIC'S APPROACH. She drew in a weak breath and blinked away the tears stinging her eyes. Why did she feel like crying? She wasn't interested in Lloyd. But she had given it her best, used every trick, and she failed.

She really thought she could have been a good decoy. She was willing to do whatever it took to catch her prey, but it didn't make a difference. Eric had been right; she didn't have the sex appeal or the street smarts.

She cast a quick glance at the exit and saw Lloyd dashing out the door. Lloyd was an honorable guy. She downed the last of her beer. He wasn't a cheater and nothing she would have said or done would have changed that. She accepted the fact, but she wished her first decoy assignment would have proven her sex appeal.

Julie discreetly removed the earpiece and clenched it in her hands. She didn't want to hear Asia make excuses for her, and she didn't want her coworkers to hear any more. They didn't need to listen to the laundry list Eric was sure to provide on how she messed up.

When Eric stood at the bar next to her, she decided to go for a preemptive strike. "I should have gone with Glamorous Julie," she said as she stared at her empty beer bottle.

"No, you made the right call," Eric said. "Lloyd wouldn't have made a move if you'd come across as unattainable."

"I went at it the wrong direction." She replayed the

conversation in her head and cringed. "I started out with something about his phone and he spent most of the time bragging about some project he did at Z-Ray."

"He was trying to impress you," he said as he placed his hand on her shoulder. "That's a good sign."

His touch felt good. She was tempted to curl against his chest, but she didn't want to show how vulnerable she felt. "Most of it was technical jargon. The only things I understood were 'revolutionary' and 'game-changer.' I still have no idea what he does."

"It doesn't matter. We came here to see if he would take the bait and he didn't. That's all we need to know."

Julie propped her chin on her fist. "I used everything in my playbook," she admitted. "I didn't even get a nibble."

"Not from where I stood. The guy showed an interest."

"I played it too careful. I was so worried I was going to break the momentum when I should have pushed."

"No, you played it cool."

"I kept looking at Blondie and Red over there." She glanced where the women were wrapped around Lloyd's friends. "Those men took the bait. They're practically having sex right now."

Eric gave a comforting squeeze on her shoulder. "You shouldn't compare yourself. Blondie and Red obviously have their own agendas. And so did those guys."

"I should have followed their lead." It went against her instincts with Lloyd, but it would have gotten the results she wanted.

"No."

She closed her eyes. Right. Her overtures would have

paled in comparison with those women right next to her. Eric saw that right away, and she just proved to him that she wasn't sexy. Why couldn't the floor swallow her up whole?

"Yeah—" she cleared her throat "—I don't think I could have pulled off that level of sexy."

"No, you misunderstood me."

"It's okay, Eric." She rolled the empty beer bottle between her hands. "You were right. I wasn't a good choice. I'm sorry I made you give me the job."

"I'm not."

No, he wouldn't. He knew she needed this wake-up call. The next time she wanted to break out of her cubicle, Perry would only have to mention the Lloyd incident. It would be enough to shut her up.

She truly needed this assignment to have been a success. Not just for her team, but for herself. She had waited so long for her turn. She had imagined how great she would be, how she would shine if only she had a chance for the spotlight.

The hope that always pushed her forward was gone. Now she regretted grabbing for the chance. She wished she hadn't tried to live her dream. If she hadn't tried she could still pretend anything was possible.

"I'm sorry this was a waste of time," she said.

"No, it wasn't a waste," Eric insisted. "We needed the practice."

"Well, the practice was wasted on me. I'm not doing it again." She gathered up her courage and met Eric's gaze. The kind understanding she saw in his blue eyes nearly destroyed her. "You'll need to find someone else to be a decoy. I quit."

7

QUITTING? ERIC STIFFENED. That didn't sound like Julie. She wasn't a quitter. It was a quality of hers that he admired and found exasperating in equal measures. She wanted to do anything and everything, as if she were making up for lost time. If she didn't have the skills, she got by with her drive and energy.

But now, after one try, she was going to quit being a decoy. This was what he wanted, right?

Eric saw the dullness in her blue eyes. It was as if the light—the joy—were snuffed right out of her. He wanted to protect her, but not at the cost of her enthusiasm.

He wasn't good at pep talks, but he'd give it a shot. "Listen, Julie…"

She released a deep breath. "I don't want your pity."

"Good, because you don't have it," he insisted. "I admit you surprised me tonight."

"I know." She tiredly rubbed her head. "The military jacket was a bad call. I took it off to show more skin, but it didn't do me any good."

"The alias worked," he insisted. "Lloyd allowed you to get a lot closer to him than Blondie and Red."

"More like Blondie and Red were already occupied."

Eric dipped his head and pressed his mouth against her ear. "I'm only going to say this once, so listen closely. You have a skill in observation. You notice signs that reveal something about a person. That takes years of training, but it's almost as if it comes natural to you."

"So, I'm a great people watcher. Big whoop." She pressed her lips together and shook her head. "I'm sorry. I don't mean to take my disappointment out on you. I appreciate that you're trying to cheer me up."

"But I suck at it?"

A reluctant smile pulled at her lips. "Something like that."

"Fair enough." He straightened and turned her bar stool so she had to face him. "I'll focus on my strengths and stick to the facts. There were no indications that Lloyd would be unfaithful to his girlfriend. Martha volunteered him. That was the only reason we chose him as a target."

Julie's eyebrows rose as she gave him a knowing look. "And because he didn't look dangerous or pose any great physical threat to me."

She knew him well. Eric was adept at hiding his feelings, but Julie could see right through his motivations. "Okay, you caught me on that. But give me a break. Next time I can't choose the target. He might be scum who'll try to get you naked before you say hello."

"I doubt we will get that lucky," she said as she reached for her jacket on the back of her bar stool. "You need to get a different decoy. Someone like Asia. If it had been Asia, Lloyd would be at the hotel next door right now, renting a room."

Eric curled his finger under her chin. He didn't speak until she met his gaze. "I don't want Asia to be a decoy. I want you," he said. "You showed that you are adaptive and instinctual. You need to develop those skills if you want to be a detective."

Julie's expression softened. "Thanks, Eric."

He stroked her jaw. Her skin was warm and smooth. He wanted to explore her face with his hands and mouth. His eyes must have given away his intentions as Julie's cheeks reddened before she pulled away.

"It shouldn't matter if he was a serial cheater or not," she said as she put on her jacket. "I should have tempted him."

"You tempted me," he reminded her. She had driven him crazy. Still did. "You made me forget all my good intentions."

She stood up abruptly. "That's different."

"Why?" he asked in a teasing tone. "Do you still think I'm an easy lay?"

"I never said you were easy," she said as she flipped her ponytail from her jacket collar.

He grasped the end of her ponytail and gave it a tug. "The assignment is finally over."

He wanted to whisk her away and relive the heat they'd shared in the supply closet. The hotel room he'd been living in was just a few floors up. All he had to do was ask.

As much as he wanted Julie, he wouldn't make his move tonight. Not when she was feeling vulnerable and had something to prove. He wouldn't take advantage, even though his primal instincts called for him to pounce. He'd wait, no matter how much it killed him.

Eric let go of her ponytail and took a step back. It was a struggle as his body wanted to gravitate closer to Julie. "Everyone on the team is meeting up at the bar in the hotel next door for a drink."

She frowned and blinked a few times as if she didn't understand what he was saying. "Why? The assignment was a complete failure."

"Were you made?" he asked. "Did Max get caught taking photos? Did the audio equipment cause any feedback?"

"No," she said slowly.

Eric shrugged. "Then that's reason enough to celebrate."

"You need to raise your expectations," Julie said with a shake of her head. "Why don't you go on ahead? I'm going to use the restroom. I'll meet you there."

"Are you sure?" He didn't like leaving her. Not when she was feeling discouraged.

"Do you really think I need an escort to the ladies' room?"

Eric raised his hands in mock surrender. "I'll save a seat for you."

JULIE STEPPED INTO THE restroom and saw her reflection everywhere. On the oversize mirrors, chrome sinks and bathroom stalls. Several women with sleek hair and tiny dresses were at the mirrors repairing their makeup and liberally applying perfume.

She entered a stall, slid the latch shut. Exhaling slowly,

Julie allowed her shoulders to sag before she leaned her forehead against the smooth metal.

That didn't go as planned. Julie closed her eyes and rocked her head from side to side. The only thing that went right was not being made as a decoy. That wasn't a major achievement to celebrate. Lloyd probably didn't think she was sexy or smooth enough to be a decoy.

Julie gradually opened her eyes and stared blankly through the door hinges. She felt numb and she welcomed it. The pain was there, just underneath, but she couldn't deal with it yet.

All this time she thought that if she had a chance, she could show off her detective and espionage knowledge. She would show everyone that her skills were wasted on tracking uniforms.

What a bunch of bull. She felt a tear trail down her cheek, but she didn't wipe it away. All of her detective and espionage skills were from books and TV. She used to think that it was okay that she was stuck in bed or in the house. She had considered it her incubation period. The moment she struck out into the world, she would be at a much higher level than any other detective her age.

That was one more fairy tale that didn't hold up to reality.

Julie rubbed her eyes. She was behind the curve and no amount of reading or studying was going to fix that. This was just like high school P.E. She was the weak link in the team. The one who dragged everyone down. The one who everyone had to compensate for by working harder if they wanted to win.

She didn't want to be a decoy anymore. What if she

failed again? Julie shuddered at the thought. If that happened, she would go back to her cubicle and never leave.

But Eric said she had skills. He wouldn't lie about something like that. He had been sweet in his blunt and gruff way, she thought with a faint smile. She liked seeing that side of him and she had a feeling he didn't show it too often.

A movement in the mirror caught her attention. The reflection showed familiar shades of platinum-blond and can't-be-natural red. She groaned and fought the urge to bang her head against the bathroom stall door. No way Kick-Ass Julie could have competed with that. She didn't care what Eric said. Big breasts trumped observation skills every time.

She was about to step away from the door and wait until the women left when she saw Blondie whip out a thin black cord from her teeny-tiny purse. Julie frowned and looked closer. Was this some new makeup tip she needed to know about? She could use all the help she could get.

Julie dismissed the possible makeup tutorial when Blondie plugged the cord into her cell phone. She then connected a USB stick onto the other side of the cord.

"I forgot my cord," Red said as she looked through her long rectangle clutch. "I need to use yours when you're done."

Blondie huffed irritably. "How the hell could you forget something like that?"

Red shrugged and the glitter coating her skin reflected in the mirror like diamonds. "It must be in the purse I used last night."

"The cord is the one thing you need. I'll loan you mine but this is the last time."

What was going on? Julie pressed her face against the door and watched the two women. They didn't look like students or women who worked for a living. So what was the urgency of backing up some files? And why would they do it in the bathroom of a nightclub?

"I'm done. Hold on." Blondie unplugged the USB stick and Julie heard the unmistakable sound of jangling keys. She squinted to get a look at the key ring. She couldn't see anything until Blondie grabbed the keys in her hand as she gave the cord to Red.

There was an action figure on that key ring. Julie drew back in surprise. It looked just like Kick-Ass Julie. It was the same action figure that had been on Lloyd's shirt.

It didn't make sense. Blondie was the kind of woman who would have Swarovski crystals on her key ring. Maybe Hello Kitty if she was feeling playful. But the charm would have to be encrusted with diamonds to meet Blondie's expectations.

"Hurry up," Blondie said impatiently.

"There's only so much I can do," Red said, tapping her sling-back pump on the tile floor. "I swear all the gigabytes are full on this thing."

Julie's eyebrows rose. It sounded weird hearing the word *gigabytes* coming out of a mouth covered in frosted pink lip gloss.

Blondie turned to the mirror and fluffed her hair with her fingers. "If they realize they don't have their keys…"

"It's going to be fine."

Oh, my God. Were they downloading the guys' information from their USB sticks? Julie pressed her face closer and tried to get a glimpse of the key ring Red held. She couldn't see it because Red had her back turned to her.

"Done." Red ripped out the cord and gave it to her friend. "Now I'm with the one wearing the white shirt, right?"

"Tell me you're joking," Blondie said as she stuffed the cord in her minuscule purse. "You've been slithering all over the guy for most of the night and you don't remember which one you have?"

"What can I say? All geeks look alike," Red replied as they walked toward the door. "Hey, wouldn't it be funny if we accidentally switched keys?"

"Don't even try it."

Julie waited a few moments until she was certain the women had left the bathroom before she unlatched the door. So that was why Blondie and Red were all over Lloyd's friends. It was as if a piece of the puzzle had fallen into place.

At first she thought they were looking for rich guys. They were hunting for someone who could buy them expensive drinks and maybe a fancy meal. It was a common myth in the Seattle area that all computer programmers were multimillionaires.

But those women could have had their choice of any man in the club. Julie bent her head as she walked out of the bathroom and made her way through the maze of people. Blondie and Red were sex goddesses and they knew it. They could have sophisticated men. Hot men. Men like Eric.

Julie clenched her teeth at the thought and powered through the crowd. She would have hated it if one of those women had set their sights on Eric. Julie knew she wouldn't have been able to compete, but she wouldn't have been able to sit back and watch, either.

But Red and Blondie didn't even look at Eric. Their full concentration was on the computer nerds. And now she knew why. It was because they were after the USB sticks.

It was weird, Julie decided as she exited the club. The women didn't grab the sticks and go. They were giving them back. Because they didn't want the computer programmers to know that the information was compromised.

Julie suddenly realized she was on the sky bridge that would take her to the hotel. She was on autopilot as she wondered what was on the USB sticks.

It couldn't be that important. Most guys who worked on computers had USB sticks on their key rings. Lloyd had one, right next to his library card.

She remembered how Lloyd had absently twirled the keys on his fingers as he bragged about his work. Revolutionary, he said. The project he was working on was a "game-changer."

Julie quickened her pace. The competition would pay a very good price to get their hands on that intellectual property. She may have seen something big. Something that was way better than premarital screening.

If only she understood what Lloyd was actually working on! She'd make up for that later. Julie picked up the pace, her boots ringing against the ground. Right now she couldn't wait to tell Eric and the team what she'd stumbled upon.

Julie was out of breath when she arrived at the bar in the hotel lobby. It was quiet and dark. She found the team sitting at a cluster of tables, toasting to their first assignment. She barely heard Martha telling everyone that she always knew Lloyd was a good guy when she rushed to the table.

"Guess what?" Julie interrupted excitedly. She felt the excitement coursing through her veins. "I just stumbled on corporate espionage."

Everyone fell silent and stared at her.

"Uh-huh," Max said as he saluted Julie with a tilt of his long-necked beer bottle. "Sure you did."

"I'm serious." Julie flattened her hands on the table top. "Do you remember the blonde and the redhead who were all over Lloyd's friends? Didn't you think that was strange?"

"No," Max said bluntly. "It's why the nerds go to those nightclubs in the first place. For the girls."

"Not Lloyd," Martha said loyally. "He was probably dragged there by those guys."

"Well, Lloyd needs to keep his key ring in a safer place," Julie said. "Blondie and Red have stolen his friends' USB sticks."

"Are you sure?" Asia asked.

"Well, they only had the sticks for a few minutes, I'm sure those guys have them back now. The guys kept their USB sticks on their key rings."

"Most programmers do," Ace, their resident computer expert, said from down the table.

"Wouldn't the information be encrypted?" Asia asked.

Ace shook his head. "Not always. People get lazy."

"I don't know if it was encrypted," Julie said. "All I know is that the women were downloading the information on their cell phones." She looked at her colleagues. "So, what now? What are we going to do about it?"

"Um…nothing," Asia said, giving Julie a curious look.

"Really?" Her friend's response stunned her. She thought Asia would be the first to jump in and develop a strategy. Asia was just as hungry for a big case. "Why would you say that?"

"Well, first, it's not a paying job. I don't do pro bono work. Second, we don't know the victim or the culprit. And third—"

"And it probably didn't happen," someone at the table said in a stage whisper.

Julie looked around the table. "It did happen."

Ace gave a chuckle. "You're just like every rookie I've seen, Uniform Girl."

Rookie? Uniform Girl? Julie glared at the guy. "What are you talking about?"

"It's like when an intern starts practicing medicine," Max explained, "and thinks they discover a rare disease. You had your first assignment and now you see crime wherever you turn."

Was that what she was doing? Seeing a big case, a potential crime, where there was none? Julie gave a quick look at Eric. He was listening to her, but didn't ask any questions. He remained watchful and quiet.

"It happens to everyone," Martha said as she set

down her cocktail. "When I first started out, I thought my neighbor was trying to poison his wife. They still won't talk to me."

"This is different. I saw them with key rings."

"They were probably *their* key rings," Ace said. "Did you consider that?"

"I did and I know the keys weren't theirs. They said they were putting them back." She clearly remembered hearing that. Her mind wasn't playing tricks. "Anyway, they seem the type to have Chanel or Coach key rings. Not something with action figures."

"They were probably updating their Facebook statuses," Martha said with a dismissive wave of her hand. "Lloyd is always doing something like that. As I was saying, Lloyd…"

Julie saw her colleagues, one by one, turn their attention to Martha. They didn't believe her. She stood straight as she glanced around the tables. No one was interested in what she saw. They thought she was imagining all this.

Julie slowly walked to the empty chair next to Eric. When he stood up to help her into her seat, she forced a polite smile on her mouth. When she sat down, she saw that Asia was on her other side.

"Asia," she whispered, "I know what I saw."

Her friend patted her hand. "Honey, is it possible…"

"What?" She was wary of her friend's cautious approach.

"Perhaps…" Asia tried again. "Could it be that your deductive skills are on hyperdrive right now?"

Her words almost sounded complimentary. Almost. "What does that mean?"

Asia twisted in her seat and lowered her head so she could speak privately. "Tonight was very important to you but your assignment didn't go as planned. You want to end the night on a successful note and just happen to see a potential case. Not just any case, but one that deals with espionage."

Wow. Julie stared at her friend, but no words came out of her mouth. She thought if anyone believed her, it would be her friend. She didn't see that one coming.

Asia gave her an apologetic look before she turned back to listen to Martha. Julie knew it was hard for Asia to give her the hard truth. Her friend knew how important the decoy assignment was for her, and how much she needed it to work.

Julie stared at her clenched hands as the conversation grew to a low buzz. Was she so desperate for a successful night that she saw something where there was nothing? She replayed the episode in her mind.

No, she was right. She saw something. She didn't quite understand it, but her gut instinct said it was a piece of a bigger puzzle. Something illegal, possibly nefarious. *Oooh, wouldn't that be great?*

She trusted her gut. That should be enough for her. She'd dig for the truth alone. She didn't need backup. Let the others think she's on a wild-goose chase. She'll prove them wrong.

Julie sensed Eric's gaze on her. She looked up and saw him watching her intently. Like he knew exactly what she was thinking.

"You don't believe me, either, do you?" she asked with a wry smile.

"Oh, I believe you."

"Really?" She sat up straight in her chair. "You think I saw something that was espionage or piracy?"

"Yeah, it's possible," he said wearily.

"Thank you." Eric believed in her instincts, her observation skills. He didn't think it was her imagination or wishful thinking.

"Promise me something." His tone was low and urgent.

"Okay, what?" she whispered.

"Don't pursue it."

Her lips parted in surprise. He couldn't possibly ask for that kind of favor. "I—but I…"

"I know that look in your eye. I can practically hear your mind buzzing. You want to investigate."

"Well…" *Duh.* Of course she did. It was her case. Her chance to show what she could do. But she couldn't share her thoughts with Eric.

His expression was forbidding. "I'm not going to let you."

Let her? As if he had a say in the matter. Let her, as if he was in charge. Her eyes narrowed. "Excuse me?"

Eric's eyes glittered as he returned her glare. "In fact, I'm going to do everything in my power to keep you away from trouble."

8

Eric didn't say any more about the subject until the team had called it a night. Most of them were tired but still giddy from working an assignment. Julie, however, was unusually quiet.

At first he thought she was subdued because her debut as a decoy hadn't met her expectations. But he'd slowly become aware of the signs. The twinkle in her eye. The secret smile. She was constantly moving even though she was sitting down.

She wasn't listening to what was going on around her. Her mind was buzzing as she planned her next move.

That was as far as he would allow.

He rode the elevator with Julie and the team. As they walked into the parking structure, he waved goodbye to his coworkers and followed Julie to the parking lot elevators. It was only when they were in the elevator riding up to another floor that Julie noticed something was odd.

"Aren't you staying at this hotel?" she asked as the elevator chimed and the doors opened.

"I'm walking you to your car."

"Thank you, but there's no need," Julie said as she exited the elevator, her stride powerful, her ponytail swishing from side to side. "It's Bellevue. Not Beirut."

"Don't knock Beirut. It's one of my favorite cities." He walked at her side, automatically scanning the area. The lot was full but quiet.

"I can take care of myself."

"Kick-Ass Julie is an alias, not a bullet-proof shield." She acted tough in her boots and military jacket, but he'd seen her self-defense maneuver. He didn't like the idea of her here alone. No one would hear her if she needed help. "Anyway, we need to talk. You are not investigating what you saw tonight."

She made a face. "Of course I am."

Why wasn't he surprised? "This is what you do— those guys work with Lloyd. You contact them or security at Z-Ray, tell them what you saw and you drop the matter."

"Where's the fun in that?"

"You may think these women are no match for you—" He heard a tire squeal and looked around, but it was from the floor below.

"Red was kind of ditzy. Blondie looked like she would fight dirty, but I could take her."

"Don't underestimate those women," Eric warned.

"Just like our colleagues shouldn't underestimate me."

"They were collecting data for someone powerful who has resources."

Julie stopped and looked straight into his eyes. "Eric, you know that what you're saying isn't warning me off. You're making it sound better and better."

He should have considered that. If there were even a hint of danger or adventure, Julie would sign up. He had been like that once. He still was when it came to Julie. She played havoc with his senses, but he was still drawn to her. He had to be around her, even though he knew he couldn't rely on his self-control.

Eric admitted he had to change tactics. "And just when do you expect to investigate?" he asked, his voice echoing against the concrete walls. "You work during the days and you'll have decoy assignments at night."

Julie stopped and placed her hands on her hips. "Why do I get the feeling that you're going to make sure I have a decoy assignment every night of the week until I drop this matter?"

Eric couldn't help but laugh. "Your faith in my abilities is gratifying, but I'm not a magician. If I could land some business for us, we wouldn't do the premarital screenings."

She bit her lower lip. "You believe there's been a theft, and you think someone should look into it. The only reason you don't want me to investigate is because you think the person should have expertise."

"Yes," he said with a sharp nod. "That's what I'm saying."

Julie grabbed his arm. "Then come with me."

"Me?"

Her eyes glowed with excitement as she warmed up to the idea. "You're an expert."

"Not in corporate espionage." Eric would do anything for Julie. He wanted to be at her side, especially to keep her safe, but this wasn't his expertise. "I hunt down and retrieve stolen artifacts for the government."

"Theft is theft," she said with a careless shrug.

Eric rubbed his forehead as he felt a headache coming on. "That's an oversimplification. A jewel thief has different methods and tools than someone who is committing a crime with a computer."

"They might use different tools, but all we need is a cell phone, a cigarette lighter and a pocketknife."

He stared at her. "Where do you get this information?"

"Books and TV. The spy always has these things with them, even if he doesn't smoke. Everyone knows that."

Eric stared at her. "Tell me that you're joking."

"I might be," she said with a smile. "And thieves might have different methods, but they're driven for common reasons." She started ticking them off with her fingers. "Greed, envy, revenge, the need for attention…"

"They also can be violent," Eric said, "which is enough reason for you to stay out of it."

"Come on, Eric. Don't you want to right some wrongs? Fight the good fight?" She pumped her fist up in the air like a superhero. "Save the day?"

"No."

Her eyes widened and she lowered her hand. "Seriously?" She stared at him. "But you…you're a…"

"Special agent. For ICE. Yeah, I know." He speared his hand in his hair and sighed, not sure if he wanted to share his world with Julie. "Let me tell you a secret about fighting crime."

Eagerness flashed in her eyes and she leaned in closer. "What? What is it?"

"Sometimes the bad guys win."

Her eyes narrowed as she waited for more.

"And sometimes you have to get on their level and fight dirty to catch them," he said slowly, his heart pumping hard. He couldn't look at Julie. "Once you do that, you'll never feel clean again."

"You will do whatever it takes," she said as she looked at him with adoration…which he didn't deserve. "It's worth it if it brings justice in the end."

"Not always." Didn't she get it? He could be just as bad, just as dirty as the thieves he captured. "Sometimes you can put together a great case, but it's not enough to convict. And if they are convicted, there's a chance that they will serve less time in jail than it took for you to put them in there."

"But you stopped them," she insisted. "That's what's important. Justice was served."

"Temporarily," he pointed out. "Don't forget that the bad guys will always outnumber you. They become stronger, richer and more dangerous every day."

"So, why do you keep at it?" Julie asked. "If you hadn't been injured, I'm sure you would still be at it, catching bad guys. Why haven't you given up?"

There had been plenty of times when he felt burned-out and useless. Days that tested his ideals. Days when good and bad wasn't black and white. He had given his youth, his body and soul, to the job and lately he didn't think it was worth it. When he was first put on medical leave, he seriously considered retiring from his no-madic life. But that would mean finding a home and a place where he belonged. The idea scared him. He didn't want a repeat of his childhood.

And then he'd walked into his godfather's firm, and he met Julie. He was someone who looked for ulterior motives and found her friendliness a rare treat. She was a natural beauty while he still carried the taint of an underground world. She was bright, creative and fun. She lived in a safe and peaceful world. A world that he fought for, but it almost felt foreign to him.

But he also remembered that look in her eye when she had discovered what he did for a living. He was James Bond and Hercules wrapped into one. It was as if all his aches and scars had faded. Every time she looked at him with that mix of idealism and respect, he felt invincible.

He also felt guilty. She shouldn't look up to him or create a fantasy about what he did for a living. Sooner or later she would understand that he was no hero. Heroes were squeaky clean and virtuous. They were better than everyone else. He wasn't good enough to stand next to someone like Julie.

"I know why," Julie said quietly.

Eric stiffened. "You do?" How did she know? Was it obvious that he wanted to be the hero of her dreams? Did she see that he wanted to be honorable and civilized just for her?

She stepped closer and placed her hand on his arm. She tilted her head and looked up at him, her expression softening with adoration. "You don't quit because it's not in your nature."

His heart skipped a beat before he relaxed. "Yeah, sure. Right."

She gave him a curious look. "What did you think I was going to say?" she asked as she let go of his arm.

"Uh, nothing. We'll go with that."

"I know that if someone throws an obstacle in your path, you find a way around it."

That sounded like him. On a good day. He hadn't had one for a while. "How do you know that?"

"Because I'm the same way," she said as she walked away.

"God, I hope not," he muttered as he followed her. But he had a feeling that she was more tenacious than him.

"And I don't care if what I saw in the club had nothing to do with me," she said as she marched to her car. "I'm not going to let those women steal just because they're tougher than me. I'm going to stop them."

Eric understood her desire to make a difference, to stop something she knew was wrong. But she also had this view that everything would work in her favor because right was on her side. There had to be a way where she could feel like a participant without getting in the line of fire. He had to find that balance.

He saw Julie approach her light blue MINI Cooper. "This is where you parked?" He stopped in his tracks and looked around the garage. Of all the places to leave a car unattended, this would be his very last choice. "It's in a blind spot for the security cameras and there is no direct light."

"It was the first one available," she said as she took her keys out of her pocket.

"And did you wonder why?" he asked as he watched her unlock the driver's door. "Like most people would avoid it because it screams 'mug me here'?"

She turned around and faced him. "And where did you park? Under a floodlight and in front of the parking attendant?"

Eric flattened his hand against his chest. "I can take care of myself. You—" he pointed at her "—I'm not so sure about."

"Thanks." Her sarcasm was loud and clear. "And here I thought you walked me to my car because you couldn't get enough of my company."

"There's that—" he placed his hand on the car door before she could open it "—and I wanted to make my point clear. You don't have to stick your neck out to find danger. Contact the Z-Ray or contact the authorities. Let someone who is qualified pursue it."

She gave him a tight smile. "You might as well pat my head and tell me to be a good girl."

Eric didn't know why his words were getting mixed up. He never seemed to say the right thing to Julie. "All I'm asking is for you to sit this one out."

"No, absolutely not."

He placed his other hand on the car rooftop, caging her in. "Why not?"

She leaned up against the car. "Because I'm always sidelined and I'm tired of it."

"Not always," he argued. "You were a decoy tonight."

"And you know what, right up until the moment Lloyd walked away, it was fun. This time I wasn't on the outside looking in. I finally got to be a part of the game."

"And you will have a chance to play a bigger part of the game, but you have to work up to it."

"That's what I've always been told. 'Next time you can have a chance,'" she mimicked. "'Be patient. Just wait your turn.'" Sadness flickered in her eyes. "But it never happened. I didn't get a turn. It's been that way since I was a child. My family didn't allow me to do anything and it's still true today."

"I'm sure your parents had good reason." He had no doubt that she was a curious and impulsive child who found trouble at every turn.

"Okay, sure I had some health issues," she admitted. "It's not uncommon with a premature baby. And it didn't help that I was always sick in bed or at a doctor's office."

"Health issues?" Eric studied her face. Her pale complexion gave her an ethereal beauty, and he always thought she was delicately feminine, but she was no waif.

"My parents were overprotective," she insisted.

Eric didn't say anything. He was kind of envious. He would have liked it if his parents showed any concern for him.

Julie's eyes clouded as she remembered. "All the neighborhood kids got to go outside and have fun and I was stuck watching them from my bedroom window."

That would explain the good observation skills. She had spent a lot of time watching the world go by. "What health issues?" he repeated.

"I grew out of them," she told him and sighed. "Eventually."

"Are you sure?"

Her gaze sharpened and he could tell she regretted saying anything to him. "What do you mean? I'm strong and healthy."

Eric didn't say anything. She was active and energetic at the office, exuding joy and a thirst for adventure. But this explained a lot about her air of vulnerability. He wasn't the only one who felt it. Many employees at Gunthrie S&I felt protective about her.

"Let's get something straight, Eric Ranger." She poked her finger against his chest. "I used to be defined and labeled by the challenges I faced. My parents still treat me as if I have the same medical needs as when I was a baby. I didn't like it then and I won't tolerate it anymore."

He didn't say anything. She may be strong and healthy now, but she acted as if she were indestructible. He didn't want to encourage that fantasy. That would cause more harm than good.

"You don't believe me?" She bristled with indignation. "Do you need to see a doctor's note? A blood test?"

"Well, you have a…" How could he explain that she wasn't a superhero, either?

"A what?" she asked. "An injury? Scars? No, wait. That's you." She poked him again in the chest. "And not once did I think you were weak or incapable."

A smile tugged at his mouth. "You think they're hot," he said in a gruff voice.

"Damn right, I do."

JULIE DIDN'T THINK THERE WAS any point in hiding how she felt. She still wanted Eric. More than ever. He wasn't going to be around for much longer. Two weeks tops.

But why did he treat her as if she were as breakable as a porcelain doll? She wanted to feel his heat and his raw power. She wanted a taste of his wild side, the side he felt he needed to hide from her.

Did he think she was too much of a good girl to enjoy a rough tumble? Then he was in for surprise. When she fantasized about Eric—which occurred more than it should have—she imagined him sweaty, tied up and desperate for her touch.

She flattened her hand against his chest and felt the heavy beat of his heart. "Eric, did you think I was weak when we were in the supply closet?"

His eyes glittered. "Oh, now we get to talk about it?"

"Did you think I was fragile?" she asked as she slid her hand up his chest.

"No." He leaned into her.

She enjoyed the weight of him pressing against her hips. "Powerless?"

"No."

She placed both hands on his wide, solid shoulders. "Did you think I was holding back?"

"No." He tilted his head as he considered her question. "Why would you?"

"You're an injured man."

"So?" His mouth hovered above hers.

"A man on sick leave."

His eyes darkened as he remembered her untamed response. "You weren't holding back."

"And I don't want you to hold back anymore." She

linked her hands behind his head and pulled him down for a kiss.

She was so hungry for him, but she didn't rush it. She tasted every inch of his mouth. Licked, nibbled and savored the moment before she deepened the kiss.

Eric clenched the roof of her car. He didn't touch or grab her. It was as if he didn't trust himself. He poured everything he felt into his kiss. She tasted the darkness in him and wanted more.

He wanted to claim her with his mouth but this time Julie wanted to take charge. She clenched her hands into his hair and held on tight. Eric's groan of surrender rumbled in his chest as he reached for her hips and held her close.

Eric ground his mouth against hers. His touch was fierce and wild. This is what she wanted. She wanted to feel his strength and power. She wanted to feel the depths of his desire.

Julie slipped her hands to the collar of his shirt and felt the erratic pulse at his throat. She tugged at the buttons as he captured her tongue. She sighed in his mouth when her fingers brushed against his naked chest. She felt him shiver as she trailed her hands along his abs, her fingers going over the ridge of an old scar.

She felt dizzy and wild. Only Eric made her feel that way. When he touched her, she felt weak and ferocious. Bold and shy. Wild, but at the same time, tamed. She could make him tremble, but he had just as much power over her.

The sensations whipped through her body, but she didn't fight them. She didn't want to. She just wanted to feel. Take. Demand.

Julie skimmed her hands down to his jeans and boldly flattened her palm against his rock-hard cock. Eric tensed and his breath was jagged and harsh. She flexed her fingers, enjoying the feel of him. She wanted him deep inside her, claiming her while her body claimed him.

She unbuttoned his jeans and drew down his zipper.

"Julie," he warned against her mouth.

She didn't want to stop. She wrapped her fingers around his cock and slowly pumped her hand. Eric tilted his head back and hissed between his teeth.

Julie watched his face as she stroked him. Her blood was roaring in her ears. She loved seeing him like this. On edge, off balance and unguarded. For one moment, he trusted her completely.

Eric wrapped his hand around her wrist and held her still. "Okay, Julie," he said with his eyes closed. "You proved your point."

It took a second before his words registered in her head. "What are you talking about?"

He removed her hand and hesitated before he took a step back. She immediately felt the loss of his weight and heat.

"You wanted to prove that you had power over me," he said as he zipped up his jeans. "So, congratulations. You made your point. But don't think that this changes my mind. I'm not going to help you."

She flinched at his words. "That is not why I kissed you."

He held his palms up. "I have done my best to keep my hands off you tonight."

"I didn't ask you to." She needed to feel his hands

on her body. Her skin. She needed his touch like she needed her next breath.

He looked down at his feet and rubbed the back of his neck. "I know you needed some…reassurance after what happened with Lloyd."

Julie's jaw dropped and she felt a blush zoom up her neck before flooding her cheeks. "This had nothing to do with Lloyd."

"And now you need to show that you have power over me." Eric looked into her eyes. "I want you badly, so much that I can't think straight. But that doesn't mean I'm going to let you run right over me."

"I don't need any reassurance." She hated how her voice shook. "Not from you. Not from anyone. And what just happened here was because I wanted it to happen."

"Why did it happen?" Eric asked. His eyes were dark with suspicion. "You want a little adventure, is that it? A walk on the wild side? I'm not against it, but we both know I'm not your type."

"True," she said angrily. "I like a man who takes action and I got tired of waiting for you to make the first move."

"You don't even want to talk about it."

"Because I know what you're going to say." She forcefully pulled her car door open. "That you're sorry and it was a mistake."

"I *am* sorry and it *was* a mistake."

Julie wanted to roar. Scream. Stomp her feet. Instead, she sat down in her car and slammed the door shut.

"Eric," she said as she started the engine, "the only

thing you should be sorry for is thinking I have an ulterior motive for having sex with you."

Eric sighed. "I am sorry."

"And the mistake you made? It's believing that I need to get your permission for anything." She threw the car into Reverse and peeled out of the parking space.

9

THIS WASN'T HIS IDEAL WAY to spend a Saturday, Eric decided as he entered the nightclub. He could have spent the day with Perry, or gone through the financials for Gunthrie S&I. He would rather have spent it with Julie. If only he could find her!

Eric slowly made his way through the crowd. The music screeched in his ears and the pulsating lights made him squint. What was it about this place that made him feel old?

He wouldn't willingly enter this club, but he knew Julie would be here. And if he were a gambling man, he would bet that she was doing exactly what he didn't want her to do.

Looking over the swaying hands, Eric decided he had to give Julie credit. She was not easy to track. Whether it was by accident or design didn't matter. He was a pro and he hadn't been able to find her all day. But he knew that she would investigate Blondie and Red, and she last saw them in this nightclub.

He surveyed the room, gritting his teeth as his

frustration bloomed. The men ranged from slimy to scrawny. Some of them were dressed in T-shirts and jeans like he was, but there were a few in shiny suits with slicked-back hair.

The women looked much the same. Long straight hair, glitter on their skin and dressed provocatively. Each woman tried to gain attention by their dancing. The movements were sexual and crude. None of the women had Julie's feminine grace.

Eric gave the bar another sweep. He didn't see Julie. But she was here. He knew it.

It would have helped if he knew which alias she had chosen for the night. He saw a man on the dance floor grab an unsuspecting woman's ass. If it was Trashy Julie, he was going to get her out of here fast. If it was Almost Bare Julie, he would approach her with great caution.

Eric reached for his cell phone. He hesitated as he stared at the screen. He had called her throughout the day, but she hadn't taken any of his calls.

Of course she hadn't. He basically said she wanted sex with him to prove something. He wanted to kick himself after he suggested it, but he didn't trust the attraction between them. He couldn't imagine why someone as sweet and innocent as Julie would want anything to do with someone like him.

Eric returned the phone to his pocket and did surveillance around the dance floor. Julie wouldn't hang around the corner or in the shadows. That wasn't how she would get information. She would capture the spotlight or be in the center of the action.

One thing he could never accuse Julie of was cowardice. She was gutsy. He'd usually admire that in a colleague, but sometimes the gutsy move was showing patience or making a sacrifice. He didn't think Julie was capable of that.

The woman in front of him flagrantly gyrated her hips to catch his attention. Eric gave her a cool stare. She stopped and quickly moved away.

If only Julie had shown that kind of common sense, he thought as he walked onto the dance floor. She needed to learn not to tease him or push her luck.

A movement caught his eye in the center of the crowd. He slowly turned his head in time to find a woman moving with mesmerizing grace. Her arms were raised, her hands curved like a ballerina as she swayed to the music.

Julie.

Eric stood motionless as he watched Julie dance. She tilted her head back and grabbed the full length of her straight hair. She piled it up on top of her head as she moved to the hypnotic beat. He stared at her, wanting to sweep his tongue along the curve of her neck and taste her fragrant skin.

He fought against the pang of jealousy as she danced in sync with another man. She was the focus of many, but she didn't notice. Even from where he stood he could tell she wasn't aware of her partner. Julie was lost in the music.

Eric swallowed hard as Julie rolled her hips to the primitive beat of the drums. Her fire-engine-red dress pulled against her curves. She really shouldn't dance in that dress. It was short, tight and strapless. Every man held their breath in anticipation of a glimpse of more.

Sweet and innocent. The words mocked him. He hadn't seen this side of her, or he never allowed himself to see it. It didn't go with the image he had of Julie Kent. He would never make a move on Good-Girl Julie with her ladylike dresses and shy blushes.

But each alias revealed a side of her. She could be sophisticated or bawdy. Rebellious and mysterious. Julie wasn't pretending to be someone else. She was exploring what was hidden behind her good-girl image.

And tonight she was Femme Fatale Julie. She could seduce with just one knowing look. Enchant and hold a man spellbound. Charm him into telling his secrets.

She could do that without the makeup and the red dress, Eric decided as he cut a path through the throng. She got him talking about stuff he didn't tell his partner.

He shouldn't have told her how he felt about being a special agent. He never planned to, but he wanted her to understand what could go wrong. Instead, he shared something he wasn't comfortable with. That wasn't like him. As a child he had learned never to discuss what was going on in his home or in his life. A part of him knew Julie wouldn't use it against him, but another part of him was waiting for his words to come back and haunt him.

Eric reached Julie. Her dance partner glared at him, ready to defend his find. Eric glared right back at him and took a step closer. The other guy paled and took a step back. When Eric took another step forward, the guy melted away in the crowd.

He seized Julie's wrist and whirled her around. She gasped and wobbled in her sky-high heels. She opened her eyes and grabbed his arm as she regained her balance.

"Eric!" Her eyes were wide and she clung to him. "What are you doing here?"

"I could ask you the same." He took another close look at her dress. He wasn't sure what was keeping it from falling.

"I'm dancing."

"Dance with me," he challenged her.

Julie slid out of his grasp. "Sorry, not unless I can prove my power over you."

Eric clenched his jaw. "I already apologized for that."

"Can't hear you," she said as she drifted away.

He grabbed her wrist again and pulled her close. He refused to be distracted by her light perfume or how her soft curves yielded against his hard body. "We need to talk," he growled in her ear.

"I have nothing to say to you."

"Great, then you can listen." He escorted her off the dance floor, giving her hand a short tug when she tried to resist. He wanted to take her out of the club, but he knew she would walk right back in. Instead, he found an empty table in a dark corner where they could talk privately.

Julie wasn't pleased to see him and she didn't care if she made it obvious. She crossed her arms and leaned against the table, unaware that her breasts were about to spill out of her dress. She turned her attention to the dance floor.

"What's up with the femme-fatale alias?" he asked.

She smiled and faced him. "You think it works?"

"Yes." Julie was a seductress. She enchanted men

with her eyes and natural sensuality. The others faded in the background. "What was wrong with your other aliases?"

"I learned my lesson yesterday and I needed to look like I belonged."

She didn't belong here. Julie looked like a sex goddess and the women were her acolytes. But once she mentioned it, he noticed that Julie's hair was straighter and there was a sprinkle of glitter on her arms and chest.

"You don't recognize the dress?" she asked.

He frowned and tilted his head. There was something familiar about it, but all he could think of was how it lovingly hugged Julie's body. He knew she wore nothing underneath and he was tempted to peel the dress off her. "I think I would remember if you wore it to work."

"I would hope so. It's stunning and has an equally stunning price tag," Julie said with a laugh. "Blondie wore this last night, but in black."

The dress was unmemorable on Blondie. But he'd never forget it on Julie. "And you just happen to have it in your closet?"

"No, I scoured all the consignment stores in Bellevue today. They didn't have my size so I had to go a size smaller. I maxed out my credit card for it."

"Why?"

She shrugged and looked away.

"So you could investigate the intellectual property theft?" he said, answering his own question for her.

"Maybe I like the club and couldn't resist coming back," she said as she fiddled with her hair.

"More like you couldn't resist looking into what Blondie and Red were doing."

"That's a possibility." She twirled her finger in her hair and yanked it away. "Okay, fine. I wanted to get closer to Blondie and Red."

He sighed. "Julie."

"Come on, Eric. Haven't you ever followed a hunch? Didn't you need to investigate because you had questions? Was there ever a time when you needed to know for yourself?"

"Maybe. When I didn't know any better."

"The guys at work are right. I am a rookie and Uniform Girl. I won't get far on my own, but I want a few more answers before I go to Z-Ray."

"What happens if you tip off Blondie and Red? You said so yourself—you are a rookie."

Julie pressed her lips together and drummed her fingers on the table. "Okay, now you're just making me mad."

"That's not my intention," Eric insisted. "I want you to see how your actions can influence a chain of events."

"All I wanted to do was find the women and see what they were up to. I bet it's an ongoing scam. That's it."

"Have you seen them tonight?" He took a quick look around.

"No, which is strange," she said, her frustration thick in her voice. "They're regulars and they're usually here on Saturday night."

Eric paused and glanced at Julie. "How do you know that?"

"I asked the bartenders, the bouncers and the waitresses." She caught his expression. "Don't worry, I didn't say anything about thefts or Z-Ray."

"I'm not worried. I'm surprised that you got any details. It can often take a couple of visits before you get any information. What did you find out?"

"Not much," she admitted. "The blonde's name is Mercedes. The redhead is Tiffany."

He raised his eyebrow in disbelief. "Really?"

"Those are the names they go by," Julie said. "They live around here, hang out with geeks during the week, but they hang with a different crowd on Saturday nights."

He looked around the room again. "What kind of crowd?"

"Slick, muscular guys," she informed him. "The one who seems to be in charge of the group is Jeremiah. Jeremiah Moon or Dune. I kept getting a different answer on that. The guys wear designer suits, lots of expensive jewelry, and drive Ferraris."

"How did you find that out?" he asked.

"I talked to a parking valet, too."

"All in one night?" he asked, and she nodded. "And they offered this kind of information free of charge?"

"Yeah. I can't afford to flash some cash after buying this dress. I'm investigating on a very strict budget."

"How did you manage to get the staff to open up?"

"It's all about having a common enemy," Julie said, eager to explain. "Last night I noticed how poorly Mercedes and Tiffany treated everyone who works here. Bad attitude. Bad tippers."

"When did you have time to notice this?" He had

watched her intently and she had been focused on her assignment.

"I don't know. I noticed how they spoke to the bartender or I heard the vicious things they said about a waitress. Anyway, I decided to act like I was looking for Mercedes and Tiffany so I could kick their asses."

"And it worked?"

"It worked perfectly!" Her eyes shone with pride. "Everyone was more than happy to give me all the information I needed."

"You did all this in one night." He shook his head in wonder. "You are amazing."

AMAZING. JULIE FELT HER cheeks heat. She didn't want his opinion to matter, but it did. It was more important than what her friends or her boss thought. She wanted Eric to realize that she could be his equal. They could make a great team, if only he trusted her abilities.

Julie tried to hide how flustered she felt. She flipped her hair. "Tell me something I don't know," she said with an exaggerated drawl.

He paused for a moment, then looked uncertain. "Okay, how about this. I think I'm a bad influence on you."

Julie scoffed at his words. "I didn't get the vengeful bitch idea from you. I actually got it from a Sapphire book."

"No, I wouldn't have thought of a tactic like that, but I might steal it for a future assignment." His smile faded. "I mean, I'm no good for you."

Who would give him that idea? Did Perry say something? Or did Asia try to warn him off? She wouldn't put it past them to tag-team him with a few choice words. Those two had their odd way of protecting her. "Who says?"

"Me."

She frowned. "It's not true. Not by a long shot. Why would you say such a thing?"

"Because I'm not a gentleman."

Julie didn't expect that answer. She absently noticed that he made no apology for it. He simply stated the truth.

"I'm not a hero, no matter what you think," he added. "Hell, half the time I don't feel like one of the good guys."

She raised her hand for him to stop. "Now you're just talking crazy."

"I was like you once. I was optimistic, enthusiastic and ready to make the world a safer place."

She wasn't surprised. She still saw those qualities in him, even if he didn't. "And now?"

Eric looked away and pulled at his ear. She found the awkward movement in such a sophisticated man rather endearing. Just when she thought he wasn't going to answer, Eric said, "I only feel like that when I'm with you."

Julie's breath hitched in her throat and her heart skipped a beat. That was the most beautiful thing anyone had ever said to her and she didn't know how to respond.

Eric glanced up and scowled at her. "Don't romanticize it."

Now that was the Eric she knew and adored. Julie bit her lip to prevent a smile. "I wouldn't dare."

"I've been a special agent for years and I haven't made that much of a difference. Most of the time I feel like I'm sealing cracks to a huge problem that's about to crumble."

"But you're out there, every day, ready to fight." She knew that from how he worked the cases when he arrived at Gunthrie S&I. Eric's actions showed he wasn't in it for the glory or the adventure. He was there because he wanted to serve and protect.

Eric shrugged. "Not a lot of good that does."

"It does make a difference." It made a huge difference to her. "You're not turning a blind eye and you're not walking away, thinking someone else can deal with the problem. You keep at it, even if you think it's a losing battle. You keep fighting, no matter what."

"That's not heroic," he said, his eyes gleaming with amusement. "That's insanity."

"Heroic. Insane." She tossed her hands up in the air. "There's a thin line separating the two."

Eric's eyes darkened as his gaze lazily traveled down her body. Her heart started to thump. Her breasts felt heavy as her nipples tightened. How was it that all Eric had to do was look at her and her body responded?

"Just so you know," he said gruffly, "you drive me crazy."

"Glad to hear it. And I wasn't even trying," she teased.

"You drove off like a bat out of hell yesterday. Today you didn't take any of my calls. I spent all day looking for you," he confessed.

"To apologize?" She didn't understand the urgency, but she appreciated the gesture. "That's so sweet."

"No," Eric said, "there was something else I wanted to talk to you about."

"Oh." She reached across the table and linked her fingers with his, giving his hand a brief squeeze. "Don't ruin this."

"I won't. I'm here to help you."

"Help me?" She drew her hand away and looked at him suspiciously. "Help me what?"

He took a deep breath. "Investigate the theft and see where it leads before you talk to the authorities."

"Why would you do that? You were totally against it." And from the look on his face, he still wasn't one hundred percent for it.

"Because I know you won't let it go. You're going to keep digging and you need someone to watch your back."

She noticed his explanation wasn't accusatory or condescending. Eric accepted how she was and he wasn't going to try and pin her in or change her. Instead, he would join her. It was almost too good to be true.

"What's the catch?"

"No catch. I'm doing this to protect you."

She wasn't sure what that meant. Was it code for interfering? She'd like a partner, not a babysitter.

"Julie, you have good instincts and great observation skills. You were able to gather some information on Mercedes and Tiffany in very little time." He frowned. "You also have a talent for finding trouble."

"I don't go looking for trouble. Why does everyone keep saying that? If anything, my life hasn't had enough action." That was until Eric walked into Gunthrie S&I. The way he touched her, the way he made her feel, opened up a whole new world for her.

"I'm going to be at your side," he promised. "I want to help you develop your instincts."

"Thank you, Eric." She moved away from the table and hugged him. She liked how he wrapped his arms around her and held her close. It felt good. It felt right. "You are going to be the sexiest sidekick," she whispered in his ear.

Eric tilted his head back. "Sidekick?"

"I'm the lead in this investigation. You are more of an advisor or consultant." It was best to get that out of the way before there was any misunderstanding. "You're not going to have a problem with that, are you?"

She saw the struggle in his eyes before he came to a decision. "No, Julie. You're in charge of the investigation."

The unspoken message was clear. She wasn't going to be in charge when he took her to his bed. She would have to fight for it. The possibilities made her shiver in anticipation. She couldn't wait to challenge his authority.

"So, what's your next move?" he asked as his hands slid down the swell of her hips.

Desire pooled low in her pelvis and she rocked against him. "For what?"

"For finding Mercedes and Tiffany," he reminded her before he caught her earlobe with his teeth.

Her skin tingled under his warm breath. "Nothing," she said in a husky tone. "They aren't here."

"We could wait longer." He darted the tip of his

tongue behind her ear. The unexpected touch made her gasp.

"We could…" Her voice trailed off when Eric nuzzled her throat. "But I don't think they're going to show."

"There are one or two nightclubs in this area," he mentioned as he placed a kiss on her jaw. "Or we could look in downtown Seattle."

Julie clung to his shoulders. "I've done enough surveillance for one night," she decided.

"You're quitting?" He placed another kiss on her chin. "I just got here."

"I don't want to work anymore tonight," she said. "What do you want to do?"

His eyes held a naughty gleam. "I have an idea or two, but you may not be ready for what I have in mind."

Her eyes narrowed. He still thought this alias was only skin deep. "We'll see about that. Lead the way."

10

Eric's arm curled around Julie, his hand resting possessively on her hip. Her heart was pounding against her ribs as he opened the door to his room. Tonight she got to be a femme fatale. Tonight she would fulfill a fantasy.

He guided her into his hotel suite and turned on the lights. Julie silently observed her surroundings. It was all simple lines and cool colors. The light gray chairs and sofa were grouped next to the big windows. Pillows were piled high on the large bed. A crystal lamp sat on the uncluttered desk.

The room was luxurious, beautiful and impersonal.

Eric came from behind her. She felt his warm breath on her neck before he placed a kiss at the jittery pulse point.

"Don't be nervous," he murmured.

"I'm not," she answered breathlessly. She was excited. She was going to spend the night with the most fascinating man she'd ever met.

But she was also very aware of how average she was.

Common. Just Julie. Nervousness twisted her stomach and she tried to calm down. It was no use. She wasn't dangerous or exotic. She didn't have extensive knowledge in the sexual arts.

If only there were something personal in his hotel room! Something that gave her a little insight into Eric's innermost desires. Not only did she want to live out her fantasy, but she also wanted to give him a night to remember. She wanted to give him something no other woman could.

Eric's hand drifted to her shoulders. She loved the feel of his rough hands. He skimmed his fingers down her dress until he found the zipper at the side.

Julie licked her lips. She wasn't ready to shed her alias just yet. She needed the dress, the shoes and the attitude to maintain the role. Just for a little while longer until Eric was so hungry for her he didn't notice when she reverted back to simply Julie.

She turned and kissed Eric. Her lips teased with his mouth. As she playfully bit his bottom lip, Julie slipped her hands under his T-shirt. His skin was hot and tight. She hummed with pleasure as her fingertips glided over his ripped abs.

Eric crushed her dress in his hands. He kissed her deeply as he fumbled for the zipper. She retreated.

"Don't tease me," he said with a smile as he gathered her in his arms again.

"I wouldn't dream of it," she said against his mouth. She bunched the heavy cotton of his shirt and pulled it up. Eric raised his arms so she could strip it off and toss it on the floor.

She caressed his sculpted arms with a sense of awe.

Julie enjoyed the feel of his sinewy muscles and the soft hair on his forearms. She couldn't get enough of his masculine beauty.

But she was no match for him. She'd found that out in the supply closet. She had submitted to Eric and would do it again in an instant. Yet, a part of her wanted to be in charge. She wanted him begging and pleading.

Eric kissed her, plunging his tongue into her mouth as he boldly cupped her breast. She melted against him before she even realized it. When she tensed, Eric broke the kiss and stared intently into her eyes.

"What's going on, Julie?" His eyes darkened and he loosened his hold. "You're acting as if you're scared of me."

"Scared? No way!" How could Eric think that? When she was with him, she felt safe and uninhibited. There was no other place she'd rather be than in his arms.

"I'll be gentle," he promised. "Nothing like last time."

Her heart ached when she saw the regret in his eyes. She didn't want him to hide or temper his responses. She wanted Eric to bare everything to her. "Last time was perfect," she said as she brushed her lips against his. "It was everything I dreamed about."

He didn't return the kiss. "Then why are you hesitating?"

"It's just that…" She didn't want to highlight her shortcomings, but she knew she would have to confess her fears to avoid any misunderstandings. "Once my clothes are off, it's just me. No slinky outfits. No sexy aliases."

Shock flickered in his eyes. "You think I'm attracted to your aliases?"

"Yes." It wasn't easy to say the word. She felt extremely vulnerable and her face grew hot.

He stared into her eyes. She wanted to look away, but she couldn't. Eric cupped her jaw and grazed his thumb over her kiss-swollen lips. "Why would you think that?"

"You didn't really start to notice me until I used the aliases," she said in a mumble.

"That's not true," he said as he pressed his thumb gently against her bottom lip. "I noticed you the second I walked into that office. But I had promised myself that I wouldn't make a move on you."

"And what changed?" she asked. "The aliases, that's what."

"No." He dragged his thumb down on her lip. "You made a move on me. I didn't expect that."

"Oh…" She exhaled slowly as she remembered how she had seduced him with her good-girl charms. No extra makeup or change of clothes. She had drawn him close and took the initiative. Within seconds she'd had him right where she wanted him.

"And when you did, you weren't using an alias. You were a mix of sweet and sexy. Naughty. Nurturing." His gaze softened as he remembered. "It knocked me off balance."

"It did?" Julie wanted to hear that. She needed to know that she wasn't the only one who was caught in this web.

"You were brazen. Daring." He dipped his thumb into her mouth. She closed her lips around him and sucked. A feral gleam leaped in his eyes. "I want you like that again," he confessed hoarsely.

"I want it, too," she admitted as she let go of his thumb. "But this time, I want you naked."

"Then get me naked," he said with a sly grin.

Julie leaned into Eric and placed a kiss on his throat as she let her hands roam his chest. She explored every line and angle as he kicked off his shoes. When she reached his jeans hanging low on his hips, she was so eager for him that she wanted to yank them off. Instead, she carefully dragged the zipper over his erection.

Eric's hands bumped against hers. His movements were rushed and clumsy as he unzipped his jeans, and pushed the faded denim and his boxer briefs down his legs.

"Patience," she replied as she brushed her lips against his chest, flicking her tongue against his nipple.

She caressed the compact muscles of his ass before trailing her hands along his pelvic bone. She slowly wrapped her fingers over his hard cock.

Eric slipped his hands into her hair and tilted her head up to meet his kiss.

As she caressed him with one hand, his fingers clenched her hair as a groan tore from his throat. He gave a warning bite to her lower lip until she loosened her hold. She stroked him until he couldn't get enough of this pleasure, this torture.

Eric tore his mouth from hers and dropped his hands to grasp her wrists. He was breathing hard, his skin taut across his cheekbones.

"Take off your dress," he ordered. "Slowly."

He dropped her wrists when she took a step back.

Julie stood still for a moment as she allowed her gaze to travel down his body. She watched the rise and fall of his chest, the clenching of his hands at his sides and the twitch of his cock. Her skin tingled and the throb deep in her belly intensified. She wanted to crawl all over Eric and taste every inch of him.

Julie held his gaze as she peeled the dress from her breasts. The muscle in his cheek bunched. She gave a slow shimmy as she pushed the red dress past her hips. Her heartbeat thudded in her ears as her dress fell to the floor.

She stood before him wearing a pair of red panties and her platform heels. Julie didn't want to cross her arms. Instead, she placed her hands on her hips and allowed Eric a good, long look. She should feel shy or vulnerable, but she didn't. She wasn't going to dip her head or hide her face behind her hair.

Eric's awestruck expression made her feel sexy and powerful. She stepped out of the dress. "Anything else, Eric?"

"No," he said hoarsely.

Her heart galloped as he reached for her. "What about my shoes?" she reminded him.

"Keep them on." He grabbed her by the waist and carried her to the bed, laying her in the center of the mattress.

Eric knelt over her, his hands bracketing her head. She was exposed to him and she enjoyed the spotlight. Julie stretched and arched her back, reveling in his rapt attention.

She brushed her shoe against his muscular calf. She

could do serious harm to him with the heels, but he didn't seem too concerned.

"I want to be on top."

A smile tugged at the corner of his mouth. "You'll have to fight me for it."

She pushed at his chest but he didn't budge. Now she wished she had taken the advanced self-defense course. "That's not fair—" Her next words dissolved in her throat as he took her nipple in his mouth.

Julie's spine bowed as Eric caught the tight bud between his teeth. She bucked her hips against him and extended her arms as the pleasure zipped through her veins. She was open to him. Exposed and willing.

Eric's touch slowly drove her wild until she was gripping the bedsheets and panting hard. She wrapped her legs around his waist, her shoes digging in the small of his back, as she wantonly rubbed her sex against him.

He curled his hands along the edge of her red panties and dragged them down her hips. She wanted to kick them off, rip them, but Eric got onto his knees and slowly tugged the red lace down her legs.

As he discarded her panties, Julie sat up and pushed at his chest. "My turn on top," she demanded. Much to her surprise, Eric smiled and silently laid back, his head at the edge of the mattress.

She quickly straddled his hips. Excitement swirled deep inside her as she saw him lying underneath her.

Eric wasted no time and clutched her hips to guide her slowly onto him. She tossed her head back as white-hot sensations streaked up her spine. She shivered, her skin flushing, as her body drew him in.

She rolled her hips and gasped as the intense pleasure unfurled through her veins. She rode him slowly, enjoying the stinging need that swirled low in her pelvis.

Julie rocked harder. She moaned when Eric held her breasts and the heat rippled through her. When she placed her hands over his and squeezed, she felt the tingle of it in her swollen clit.

She had to chase the pleasure. Julie rode Eric harder. Her hair fell around her face as she stared, mesmerized by Eric's expression.

He looked just as she felt. Primal. Aggressive. She tried to hold off her climax. It was too soon. She wanted this to go on forever.

Eric's gaze was intense on her eyes. His movements grew urgent, as if he knew she was on the edge. He reached between her legs and stroked her.

The hot, jagged climax forked through her. Eric thrust a final time. Her mind tumbled into a kaleidoscope of colors and sensations and she reached the pinnacle. The pleasure burned through her. She heard Eric shout out his release before she tumbled down and into the void.

A FEW HOURS LATER JULIE curled up next to Eric and watched him sleep. He lay sprawled on the bed. His arms were bent above his head. One leg dangled off the mattress as the other pinned her ankles down.

She had never seen him so unguarded. He looked younger and relaxed. Julie sighed with contentment. She splayed her hand against his chest and felt his solid heartbeat.

Julie leaned her head on his shoulder. What they

had was supposed to be a fling. A sexual escapade. She wasn't supposed to have fallen in love with him.

She squeezed her eyes shut as the truth punched at her. She wasn't even sure when it happened. It had snuck up on her. One moment she was lusting at the sight of him, then infatuated by his skills and training. The next thing she knew, her heart was full with adoration as she watched him struggle with his code of honor.

He was supposed to be her fantasy. The secret one-night stand. But behind the scars and lean muscle she discovered a man who took care of his tribe.

Eric had immediately taken charge at Gunthrie S&I so he could lift the burden from Perry's shoulders. Every day he had given his time to her colleagues and shared his knowledge so they could improve their skills. He took care of this tribe without expecting anything in return.

Falling in love with Eric Ranger was probably the most reckless move she could have made. He was a special agent who never stayed in one place. She was a woman who daydreamed about spies and villains to escape her boring job.

He was leaving in just over a week. She didn't want to think about it. They were mismatched and any relationship was doomed from the start. She knew it all along, but it didn't stop her from giving her heart to Eric.

But she had no expectations that this vacation fling was meant to last. She would treat this as a brief affair, hide her pain under a sophisticated veneer and accept the inevitable end with grace and dignity.

And that started now. She wouldn't cling or smother

him with attention. That meant she shouldn't stay the night, no matter how much she wanted to.

Julie quietly sat up and dragged her feet to the floor. She wasn't sure where she had flung her platform heels. She peered over the edge of the bed when Eric startled her by clamping his hand over her wrist.

"Leaving so soon?" His voice was rough with sleep.

"I should go home."

"Why?" He tugged at her hand. "Do you have a plant to water? A goldfish that suffers from separation anxiety?"

She laughed. "No."

"Stay," he whispered.

That was all she needed to hear for her to tumble back into bed. "I don't know if this is a good idea."

"I disagree." He rolled on top of her and settled between her legs. "I refuse to walk you back to your car when we could be here."

She stiffened. "Oh, my car! I forgot all about it. The parking fee is going to be astronomical."

His eyebrow rose in disbelief. "I'm lying on top of you—naked, I might add—and you're thinking about parking? You are hard on the ego."

"Think you can make me forget about my car?" she challenged. "Not a chance."

There was an unholy gleam in his eyes as he boldly cupped her sex with his hand. No warning, no seduction, and yet she found it incredibly arousing.

She couldn't drag her gaze away from his as he glided a finger inside her. She blushed at the sound of her moan, and Eric smiled with appreciation.

He slid another finger into her core and her hips undulated from the invasion.

"What are you thinking about?" he taunted.

She wouldn't give up that easily. "I was wondering where I put my parking stub."

"Liar," he said with a chuckle as he teased her intimately.

Her breath came out in little puffs. "I can't remember which floor I parked on."

His hand fell away. Julie groaned with disappointment. She'd pushed it too far, determined to win the challenge. She should have remembered how fragile a man's ego was.

Eric bent down and placed his mouth against her sex. Julie gasped at his audacity. Her breath caught in her throat as he flicked his tongue.

"Eric!" She grabbed his hair with her fingers. Eric knew exactly how to give her maximum pleasure. Within seconds her hips jerked and bucked against his mouth. A soft climax rippled through her.

Eric crawled up her body as sweat beaded on her hot skin. "Stay the night." It was part command, part plea.

Her arms and legs felt heavy as she curled them around Eric. "How can I say no when you asked me so nicely."

He parted her legs and pressed his cock against her. She tilted her hips in invitation. "But tomorrow," she said, "you're sleeping over at my place."

Eric froze. For one heart-stopping moment Julie thought she had made a mistake. She spoke like a girlfriend. She shouldn't have made demands on his time. She had no right.

"Your place?" he asked gruffly as he braced his hands on either side of her head. He stared at her face, looking intently into her eyes. "Are you sure?"

Julie realized her request pleased him. "Yes." She exhaled as he slowly entered her. "I might even make dinner for you."

"Dinner," he repeated.

He spoke in a daze as if a quiet night and a home-cooked meal were a deep, dark fantasy of his. If only. "Will you come home with me?" she asked in a whisper.

His forehead touched hers. "Yes, Julie," he said softly. "Tell me when and I'll be there."

_11_

ERIC RESTED HIS ARMS on the bar, struggling with the sense of déjà vu. The nightclub was dark and crowded. Music pulsed from the tiled floors and mirrored walls. The scent of perfume, alcohol and sweat filled the air. It was another Friday night, another premarital screening. Same nightclub in Bellevue, same procedure. Only this time he couldn't find their decoy.

He surveyed the area but didn't see Julie. It was strange. She enjoyed being a decoy but she wasn't honing in on the target. Sometimes he thought she had more fun preparing her alias than the actual assignment, but that could be wishful thinking on his part.

Where was Julie? He looked around again. He didn't want to spend all night at the club. He only had a few more days before he left for D.C. and he didn't want to spend it on work. He wanted to spend it with Julie alone.

He had worked hard to find Perry's agency more premarital screening assignments. It was paying the bills and there would be no layoffs for now.

He frowned as he counted how many days he had left

in the Seattle area. He didn't like to think about it, but there was no future for him here. Julie had opened her home to him and they shared all their time together in the past week, but he knew not to read too much into it.

Julie was only interested in a fling. A walk in the wild side. She didn't need any guidance, he thought with a smile, but he was glad she had chosen him. Julie Kent may look innocent, but she managed to turn him inside out.

He punched in Asia's cell phone number. The moment his second-in-command answered, Eric asked, "Where is Julie?"

"She's in the nightclub, I'm guessing."

"The target is at the bar. Julie is not." He glanced at the man in question. Zack wore a blinding white T-shirt and extremely tight blue jeans. He was slouched against the bar trying to talk up a brunette.

The wrong brunette. He should be propositioning Julie.

Eric winced. God, he couldn't believe he just thought that. "What is she doing?" he said sharply.

"Hey, I adore Julie," Asia said. "But sometimes you need to leash her. She's having way too much fun with her aliases."

"Those aliases are the quickest way to get to the target," Eric said in defense. He knew Julie placed too much emphasis on her disguises, but he was impressed by how she got into the target's head and figured out each man's particular fantasy girl.

"If I were heading this assignment, we would be celebrating at the hotel bar already."

"Asia, I promise you can lead the next premarital

screening." He wouldn't be here to take charge and if he had to transfer leadership, he would choose Asia. "Just tell me where she is."

"I want it in writing that I get lead. You know Max is champing at the bit to take charge."

He expected nothing less from Asia. Julie, on the other hand, would accept his word. She believed in him and his abilities, and he didn't take that honor lightly. "I'll send an email to Perry tonight," he told Asia.

"Thank you," she answered smugly. "I'll tell Julie to find you."

He ended the call, chugged down his water and checked on Zack's location. From the disgusted expression of the brunette and how quickly she walked away, he suspected Zack failed to get as much as the woman's name. Eric scanned the premises. This would be the best time for Julie to strike.

Where the hell was she?

He looked out onto the dance floor. Suddenly, the crowd parted. Eric blinked as he saw Julie under a spotlight, dancing to the music as she went from one partner to the next.

His heart clenched at the sight of her. Julie's appearance wasn't that different than how she looked at work. Her hair was pulled back in a tight French braid and her makeup was understated. She wore a fitted black halter dress that fell several inches above her knee. She looked sexy, but not scandalous.

She twirled on her black stiletto heels and Eric discovered that her dress was entirely backless. The plunging V showed a dramatic expanse of her smooth pale skin and suggested she wore nothing under that dress.

Eric watched, mesmerized, his pulse skipping a beat when she leaned forward. How did she keep from falling out of that dress? Sheer willpower?

As he watched her dance, he noticed the slight differences in her expression. Her friendliness was absent, and her mouth was formed in a pout instead of her breathtaking smile. He wasn't fond of her aloof manner, but he could guess her alias: Ice Princess Julie.

Soon, his gaze ensnared hers. Julie's eyes brightened and her lips pursed as if she were holding back a smile. He wanted that smile. Waited for it, but it didn't come.

Julie faced him, her hips swaying, and motioned for him to come forward. Damn if that confident curl of her finger made him get up and meet her.

He moved as if he were hypnotized. His progress was slow, but he only had eyes for her. When he reached Julie, she pressed her hand against his chest before he could wrap his arms around her and stake his claim.

"What did I tell you about your shoes?" he asked.

"Aren't they fabulous?" She twisted her foot from side to side. The metallic heel reflected the colored lights. "They were a steal at this consignment shop in Redmond."

"They put you at a disadvantage."

"No way, Eric. These shoes are my secret weapon. Look at what they do for my legs."

It was best if he didn't stare at her legs and remember how they felt tangled with his or wrapped tight around his waist. "Your target is at the bar," he said, mindful of the people around her and the earpiece she wore.

"I know," she said as she linked her arms around his shoulders and rocked her hips against him.

"The bar is that way." He pointed his thumb over his shoulder.

"I've been keeping an eye on Zack," she promised as she turned around and leaned against his chest while she danced.

"Sure you have." Was she trying to drive him crazy?

"He only goes for women who blew off other men," she said as she rocked her hips against him. "Hotter, cuter men. It's like a challenge for him."

"You saw that from across the nightclub?"

"Yes." She turned around and hooked her leg over his hip. "The dance floor offers me a great vantage point before I make my move. My guess is that he has something to prove, but I can't tell if he would go with a woman who—" She stopped in midsentence as her eyes widened.

Eric immediately went on alert. "What's wrong?"

"I see Mercedes and Tiffany at the bar," she said excitedly. Julie frowned and tilted her head as if she were listening to voices in her head. "No, Asia. They aren't relevant to the case. Not this case, anyway."

"Are they moving in on Zack?" Eric asked. The last thing they needed was to have to compete for their target's attention.

"I doubt it." She peered over his shoulder and tracked the women's movements. "They go for computer geeks in pairs."

"Then focus, Julie."

"Oh, I'm focused." Her eyes narrowed into slits.

Eric grasped her upper arms and looked directly into her eyes. "On our case," he clarified. "The one we're getting money for so we can pay the rent."

"But…but…" Her eyes flashed with frustration. He knew she was conflicted. She wanted to redeem herself with the decoy assignment, but the other investigation was so much more enticing with a bigger payoff.

"I'm going to make it very simple for you," Eric said. "Whatever you're thinking, the answer is no."

Her mouth set into a firm line. "You don't even know what I'm considering."

"Yes, I do. You want to do the decoy assignment and investigate at the same time."

Her shoulders sagged in defeat. "How did you know that?"

"Finish this assignment first." He saw the rebellious flare in her eyes. "That's an order."

"Fine. I will. Oh, and don't take what I'm about to do personally. It's part of my alias, I swear." She flattened her hands against his chest and pushed him away. He staggered back a step and she flounced off the dance floor.

Eric watched her leave, enjoying the sight of her bare back. He couldn't wait to take her back to his hotel and strip the dress from her body.

He frowned as he watched Julie stride past Zack. Was it his imagination or did her hips wiggle a little more? It caught Zack's attention. The man watched Julie's ass as she bent down to adjust her shoe before taking a bar stool several seats away from her target.

What was she doing? Eric walked off the dance floor ready to correct Julie's mistake. He watched her request an apple martini. As she waited for her order, she gave Zack a quick once-over. When Zack raised his glass in a salute, she casually dismissed him.

Eric winced. This night was not going as planned. What was wrong with Julie? She could wrap this Zack around her finger if she wanted to. Was she trying to blow the assignment so she could pursue Mercedes and Tiffany? He wouldn't put it past her.

He saw Zack get up from his bar stool. Great, the guy was probably going to leave and they had nothing for their client. No audio, no photos, no evidence. Nothing.

This was why he could never trust Julie as his partner. She wanted excitement and most investigations were mind-numbing work. She got distracted with whatever was new and shiny and wouldn't have his back.

He should have known better than to give her a second chance. It had been a moment of weakness.

Eric's mouth sagged open as Zack moved in on Julie. He couldn't see what the guy said. Julie had a bored look on her face as she shrugged and gestured at the seat next to her. Zack gratefully sat down.

Wow. She knew exactly how to manipulate Zack. He had been wrong about Julie. Perhaps she didn't need his constant supervision. Maybe he should give her a little leeway.

He saw her attention divert to Mercedes and Tiffany. *Or maybe not.*

"So?" Zack drawled, his mouth too close to her ear for comfort.

Julie jerked her head back and swatted his hand as he slid his fingers under her dress. The guy was getting bolder with every minute she stayed. "I'm sorry?"

She compulsively snuck another look at Mercedes

and Tiffany. They definitely followed a procedure. She knew that in a few minutes they would visit the restroom to download information onto their phones.

She wondered if the two unsuspecting computer geeks they were with were employees of Z-Ray. Nothing on their T-shirts revealed where they worked. All she could tell is that the men looked as if they had won some cosmic jackpot.

"Come on, baby. What do you think?" Zack asked with a knowing laugh.

She wrinkled her nose at the smell of alcohol. What did she think? She thought their client was wasting her money and time on this louse. Zack wasn't worth the trouble. "Think about what?"

He licked his lips as he stared at her chest. "Let's go somewhere private."

It was amazing. She hadn't been kind to Zack and practically ignored him as she did surveillance on Mercedes and Tiffany. Yet he thought she was ready to jump into bed with him. The man was delusional. "Where do you suggest?" she asked.

"There's a classy hotel next door."

Julie shook her head, dismissing the idea. "I hear there's a conference going on. No way could we get a room."

Zack pulled out a hotel key card from his jeans pocket with a flourish. "I have one," he said with a triumphant grin.

She didn't expect that. "Well, aren't you prepared?"

"Let's go," Zack said as he stood up.

She heard the crackle of static in her ear before

Asia spoke. "Okay, Julie, I think we have enough. Wrap it up."

"I'm sorry, Zack, but you're just not my type." She looked over his shoulder and her gaze clashed with Eric's. "I like to tie up men and then lick every inch of them."

Zack looked as if he was going to swallow his tongue.

Asia hooted with laughter. "Do you really think that's going to make him back down?"

"I'm into that," Zack insisted as sweat beaded on his upper lip.

"Ri-i-i-ight." She drew the word out. "You look like a beginner. You wouldn't last an hour as my sex slave."

"Sweetie," Asia's voice crackled in her ear, "you just challenged his masculinity. We need to talk about how to repel a man."

Zack slid his hands over her legs and cupped her ass. "Believe me, babe, I could last all night."

"Good to know." She saw Mercedes and Tiffany head for the restroom. Time was of the essence. "But first I need to make a phone call to my parole officer."

Zack withdrew his hands. "P-parole officer?"

"It's no big deal," she said as she backed away. She couldn't tell if the women had taken a couple of USB sticks or not. "I found out this guy I was sleeping with had a girlfriend. I kind of went all *Fatal Attraction* on him."

"What?" His voice was a high squeak.

"That's good, Julie," Asia encouraged her. "Nothing freaks a man out more than a bunny boiler."

"Oh, and I need to make a quick stop at the restroom. I have to take my antibiotics for my rash," Julie announced. "I'll be right back."

She hurried to follow Mercedes and Tiffany. "Asia, do you think we have enough? I don't think he'll still be there when I return."

"We have enough. If the pictures of how he kept grabbing you don't do it for the girlfriend, the hotel key card should be enough evidence that he planned to cheat."

Julie glanced over her shoulder. "Oh, look at that. Zack is already making his escape."

"And Eric is calling me," Asia said. "I bet he wants to know what you said to Zack that made him run."

"Tell him to use his imagination," she suggested. "I'm going to take out my earpiece and turn my phone on now."

"You did great, Julie. I'll see you in the hotel bar to celebrate."

"Thanks." She slowly removed her earpiece and dropped it in her tiny evening purse. As she stepped into the restroom and approached the mirrors, she thought about what her friend had said.

She got what she came for. She showed her colleagues that she could do the job. She got her target using strategy and a sexy alias. So why wasn't she pumping her fist in the air and doing a victory dance?

Last week she had been disappointed when she didn't entrap her man. Tonight she didn't have anything to prove. She trusted her observation skills and her instincts. But it was more than that. She felt powerful and sexy.

Her confidence wasn't from her alias. When she was

around Eric, she felt strong and desirable. She was at the top of her game because he brought out the best of her.

Julie fished in her purse for her cell phone. She turned it on, wondering how many messages she'd received from Eric when she saw Mercedes and Tiffany out of the corner of her eye.

She looked at her phone and then at the women as an idea popped into her head. Forget protocol. Why investigate when a picture said a thousand words?

Mercedes and Tiffany were huddled together, their heads bent over their phones. She couldn't tell if they were connecting the USB sticks to their phones or if they were simply texting. She needed the right angle to get a good picture of the women and what they were doing.

Julie quietly positioned the cell phone. She tried for a tight shot of their faces and the phones in their hands. She pushed the button.

The camera flash went wild. It reflected on the mirror, the bright tiles and the shiny fixtures.

Oh, shoot. She held the phone against her leg. *Make it stop, make it stop!*

"What the hell was that?" Mercedes whirled around and saw her. Her attention zeroed in on the phone. "Were you taking pictures? Of us?"

"In the bathroom?" Tiffany asked with outrage.

"I'm...I'm so sorry." Julie watched as the women unplugged the USB sticks, stuffing phones and cords into their designer purses.

"What is wrong with you?" Mercedes took a threatening step toward her.

She had to come up with a convincing excuse. Julie

went with the first thing that popped in her head. "I love the dress you're wearing."

Mercedes, Tiffany and Julie stared at the tiny velvet dress that had a bold mix of patterns and animal prints.

Julie nervously licked her dry lips as she took a cautious step back. "I wanted to take a picture for the next time I go to the thrift store."

"The thrift store?" Mercedes' face turned red with anger. "I'll have you know that this is Versace."

"Huh. You don't say. Well, that's way out of my price range."

"No kidding." Tiffany gave a disparaging look at Julie's dress as they walked past her. "Now get your thrift-store ass away from us."

"All right. All right." She raised her hands in surrender. She didn't want them to take her phone or start a fight. "I didn't mean to upset you."

Julie watched the two women march out of the bathroom before she slumped against the mirror. She felt shaky, almost nauseated, as her blood pumped hard through her veins.

That had been a close one. Still, the next time she was cornered, she would know to act like a dumb party girl with a taste for designer clothes.

She wasn't sure where she came up with that strategy. Definitely not the Sapphire books. Maybe she was getting better at this. Julie slowly smiled as she started to follow. Today a decoy, tomorrow a private detective.

ERIC HELD BACK AS HE watched the door to the women's restroom. He was concerned when he saw Julie follow

Mercedes and Tiffany. It was a simple surveillance maneuver, but he couldn't back up Julie.

When Mercedes and Tiffany returned to the bar, he noticed their expressions. He knew Julie had made a move. A confrontation? A mistake? Eric couldn't tell. He knew the redhead was angry. The blonde had a haunted look in her eyes.

That was never good. A pursued criminal was a dangerous creature. Unpredictable, violent and defensive.

He didn't see Julie anywhere. It was difficult to determine if she was keeping a safe distance or if she was in trouble. Eric was about to storm into the women's restroom when he saw Julie. His relief was short-lived. Eric saw the determined set to her jaw and her gaze was focused intently on the women.

Every instinct warned him to go for Julie. She was being ruled by her emotions. He needed to get her out of there before she made a scene.

He moved for her. The music and voices faded as the beat of his heart pounded in his ears. Everything felt as if it was going in slow motion. Eric saw Julie raise her hand. Only then did he notice the cell phone.

Eric checked the position of Mercedes and Tiffany. The redhead was kissing a man, her hands all over his body. The blonde was a little more reserved. He saw her put her hand in the guy's jeans pocket.

Mercedes was returning the guy's key chain just when a bright flash reflected against the chrome and glass.

Mercedes whirled around and he knew the moment she saw Julie. The look in the blonde's eyes made him lurch into action.

He reached Julie but he sensed Mercedes approach. He grabbed Julie by her shoulders and pushed her in the direction of the exit. "Go, go, go!"

"I got it!" she squealed excitedly.

"I know." He saw the quickest route to the exit and slalomed through the crowd. "Mercedes and Tiffany know. The whole damn nightclub saw you take that picture."

"And I got one in the bathroom while they were downloading the information."

"Of course you did." They burst through the doors of the nightclub and looked around the empty mezzanine. He considered his choices.

They needed to hide. Fast. "Take the back stairs."

Julie scoffed at the idea. "In these shoes?"

He was already rushing her past the elevators. "I have a bad feeling those women aren't working alone. They have people watching out for them."

Her gasp rang against the pale marble that surrounded them. "Why didn't you tell me this?"

"It only just occurred to me." He should have considered the possibility immediately. "They're coming after us and they will split up to find us. They'll first go for the most obvious places."

"The stairs are the slowest way out of here."

"Which is why they'll spend most of their resources on the escalators and elevators."

"Okay, okay. We'll take the stairs." She kicked off her shoes, scooped them up in her hands and followed him barefoot.

He found the stairs in the far corner of the building.

He raised his head when he heard footsteps. He motioned for her to go up to the next level.

"Where are we going?" she whispered.

"To my room."

She shook her head. "We should go to the hotel bar. Everyone is waiting for us and there's safety in numbers."

"The less Mercedes and her gang know about our colleagues, the better." He placed his hand against her back and encouraged her to move faster.

"So, we're hiding out?" Her face lit up as she gave a brilliant smile. "This is so exciting!"

Eric looked over his shoulder. "Not if they catch us."

12

ERIC HURRIED JULIE into his hotel suite. From the corner of his eye he saw Julie fling her purse onto the table and toss her shoes underneath. He checked the hallway one last time to make sure they had not been followed.

He shut the door and locked it. When he slid the security bolt home, he didn't feel any relief. If anything, he felt cornered. Trapped. Hiding wasn't his usual strategy. He pursued and attacked.

His blood pounded and every instinct called for him to hunt down the enemy. But he couldn't take the risk. He had Julie to protect. He had to hide her as far away from the danger as he could.

Eric leaned back against the door and found Julie smiling as she twirled around the room with her arms outstretched.

He shook his head. Unbelievable. "You're enjoying this?"

Julie stopped to hug him. "Absolutely! Aren't you?"

"I'd rather chase than be chased," he said, but from the glow on Julie's face, she didn't have a preference as long as she got to be in the game. "They know you took pictures of them."

"Wasn't that great?" Her eyes sparkled. "If only I knew who they worked for."

The idea of her investigating more made his blood run cold. "You've done enough. It's time to stop poking around and give what you have to Z-Ray."

"I'm not done yet," Julie said as she flattened her hands against his chest.

He grabbed her wrists and held her hands still. "Those women know they're being watched. They know you have incriminating evidence."

"How awesome is that?" She was about to burst with joy. "They think I'm a threat. No one has thought of me as that before."

She was kidding, right? Julie had been a threat to his peace of mind ever since he'd met her. "They aren't going to take any more risks. In fact, they probably went under," he lied.

"They don't seem the type," she murmured as she leaned into him, her hips snuggled against his. "They're more of the kind who would strike when crossed."

"And yet, you went after them with no plan, no backup?" His chest tightened as he considered what all could have gone wrong. "What were you thinking?"

She rested her head against his shoulders. "I had backup. I had you."

He let go of her wrists and held her close. Eric closed his eyes and pressed his mouth against her hair. He liked that she trusted him completely. She had no doubt that he would look after her. But Julie's blind faith in his abilities made him nervous. She thought he could do anything.

"I'm not invincible," he said quietly. The scar running down his side was testament to that. "What if I didn't get to you in time?"

"I would have held them off until you got there."

Okay, now she was overestimating *her* abilities. He knew it was the adrenaline rushing through her veins. She had taken a risk and narrowly escaped. She felt powerful and violently alive.

"I want you to quit," he said. He felt her flinch and gently stroked her hair. "I'm leaving this weekend."

"I know." He felt her exhale before she moved away. "We don't need to talk about it now."

He wanted to keep holding her but he let his hands fall to his sides. "I won't be able to help when you try to pull another stunt like this."

She looked down at the floor. "Eric, you don't have to worry about me."

"Obviously, I do."

"I know that I'm no expert," she said and wrapped her arms around her waist. "I need a lot more training, and years of apprenticing before I strike out on my own."

He was glad she was aware of her limitations, but she didn't say she would back down. "So, what are you saying?"

"I'm saying that I won't pursue this once you're gone." It was a reluctant but earnest promise. "I don't want you to worry about me."

"I don't think that's possible." Her safety would always be his top concern.

"But I want to thank you." She cupped her hands against his jaw. "For believing in me. For being at my side. It meant a lot to me."

"You're welcome," he said gruffly. He didn't like the finality of her tone. As if this was already goodbye. He hadn't left for D.C. yet.

Julie brushed her lips against his mouth. He felt a wave of emotion behind the seemingly light touch.

"I love you, Eric."

He flinched. No, that couldn't be true. Julie was warm and affectionate, but she couldn't love him. He'd had relationships in the past, but they never lasted for long. Eric never wanted anyone to get too close and see why his parents couldn't love him. But Julie thought she was in love with him. What did she see that no one else could?

Eric held her by the shoulders and made her take a step back. "Julie, that's the adrenaline talking."

She frowned. "No, it's not."

"It's okay." He held up his hands. "The rush makes you do crazy things. Say things that feel true at that moment. Don't worry, I'm not going to hold you to it."

But he wanted to. He wanted to believe it was real and lasting. He knew that once Julie gave her heart, it would be forever.

"I think I know how I feel." There was a hint of annoyance in her voice. "Stop making excuses for me."

"You sound very sure of yourself. But believe me, it's only temporary. This feeling will pass."

"Is that what you want?" Her voice cracked. "Do you want my feelings to just disappear?"

Eric looked away and slowly shook his head. He

knew she would regret her declaration. One day she would discover that he wasn't the man, the hero, she needed. He didn't want to disappoint her but it was inevitable.

She placed her fingers against his mouth as he began to speak. "Eric, you don't have to love me back."

"But I..." He wanted Julie and he wanted to be with her, but his ugliness would bleed into her safe little world.

"I'm not expecting anything in return," she said, dropping her hand from his mouth. "I just wanted you to know. That's all."

That's all. Maybe Julie was used to being surrounded by friends and loved ones. She didn't realize that her words changed everything. It was a gift he didn't deserve, but he would strive to earn it.

He held her face in between his hands and kissed her. Dark, fierce emotions whipped against him. He couldn't return those words. Doing so would keep Julie at his side and she deserved better. She had a brighter future, a better life, without him.

Eric couldn't tell Julie that he loved her, but he would give her anything else.

He held her against him. His blood thickened as she yielded to him, her lips clinging to his.

"Tell me what you want," Eric said huskily. "Tell me anything and I'll give it to you."

"I want you."

Her simple words made his gut clench. "You already have me." He was hers and he always would be. "I want to give you your deepest, darkest fantasy." He could be her fantasy, her perfect man, for one night.

Eric felt her tense and he was fascinated by the naughty gleam in her eye. "Tell me."

"No, no." She ducked her head. "It's…nothing."

"It looked like something. Share it with me."

She shook her head. "You're not ready for it."

Eric was amused. He wasn't ready for it? What was Julie afraid to suggest? She should trust him and know he would give her just about anything. "I can't wait to hear this."

She rubbed her face against his neck before whispering in his ear. "I want to tie you down to the bed."

Lust scorched through his body. It zigzagged through his veins as his heart pounded. "Really?" he drawled. Julie had the incredible ability to surprise him at every turn.

"I want to be in charge," she said as she curled her arms around his back. "Tease you until you go wild."

"You've been doing that for weeks."

"You have your fantasies. I have mine."

He liked being the star of her fantasies, but light bondage was more than about sex. It was about the exchange of power. It was about trust.

How much did he trust Julie?

"I have a few ties in my closet. Go chose a few."

Julie pulled away. She bit her bottom lip before she rolled back her shoulders and tilted up her face. His heart skipped a beat as her smile grew brazen.

"No, Eric," she said softly. "You go get them."

HOURS LATER, ERIC WAS sprawled naked across the bed and Julie curled up against his side. Her skin was now cool to the touch. The bedsheets were a tangled mess at their feet and a few pillows were on the floor. He was too exhausted to reach up and turn off the lights.

"Why did you decide to spend your medical leave helping Perry?" Julie asked.

Eric frowned, not sure why she was asking him that question. "I knew he was worried about his business and I had the time to help."

"And that's it?"

He didn't need any more incentive. Perry rarely asked for help. At the time Eric thought he didn't have any special skills to help Perry grow his business, but he was willing to pitch in and do whatever was necessary. "It's better than staying at home," Eric replied.

"Something tells me you would have helped Perry even if you were busy," Julie murmured as she lazily stroked his chest.

"Yeah, I would have." Eric closed his eyes as he enjoyed Julie's caress. "It's the least I could do. Perry helped me when I needed it the most."

Her hand stopped. "When was that?"

"Long time ago when I was a kid."

"I bet you were a cute kid." Eric heard the smile in her voice.

"Not according to my teachers or the neighbors. I was a problem child and always in trouble." He tried to forget most of his childhood, but he had spent a lot of time in the principal's office and would always remember it in vivid detail. "The nicest adjectives they used were *disruptive* and *destructive*. Perry thought I was just a curious child who needed direction. That guy always had my back even when he knew I did something wrong. I could always go to him."

"That sounds like Perry." Julie's voice was husky with sleep as she burrowed her head into his shoulder. "What about your parents?"

Eric felt the tension invading his body and tried to ward it off. "They had other problems to deal with. My mom walked out on me and my dad when I was ten."

His muscles locked as the words escaped his mouth. He hadn't planned on telling that to Julie. He never discussed that defining moment in his life with anyone.

"What? That's terrible."

He shrugged and kept his eyes closed. He didn't know which was worse: his mother's absence or the toxic home environment before she left. "I used to blame myself until I got older and realized she never wanted to be a mom or a wife. She had no interest in me or in being at home. She would have left even if I had been the perfect son."

Julie was quiet for a moment. "And your dad?"

Eric released a deep sigh as the memories washed over him. "He went on a downward spiral once Mom left. He had been hospitalized several times for depression and died when I was eighteen. He couldn't take care of himself, and half the time he forgot about me. So Perry let me crash at his place most of the time."

"Why are you staying in a hotel instead of staying at Perry's?"

He was tempted to give a flippant reply about liking his privacy, but he knew that attitude was a flimsy shield against Julie's persistence. "Because the last time I camped out at Perry's I was an angry and scared teenager. I don't want to revisit that time of my life."

"I can understand that." Julie curled her arm around his chest and held him close.

Eric stilled in Julie's casual embrace. He couldn't decide whether to pull away or to enjoy her touch. "Perry gave me my first after-school job," he said in a rush, trying to conceal his discomfort.

"At his agency?" she asked with a yawn. "Weren't you kind of young?"

"At first I did odd jobs or errands. Some light cleaning." Eric slowly relaxed in Julie's arms. "Anything to get money in my pocket and food in my stomach. I was at Perry's agency more than I was at school or at home, and I started learning basic investigative skills. It turned out I was good at it."

"Why didn't you work for Perry?"

"I was going to, but Perry thought I needed more structure than he could give. He encouraged me to join the army when I graduated high school. He felt it was the only way I could make a clean break from my past. He was right."

"So, when you got out of the military, you went to work for ICE."

"I couldn't resist," he said as he stroked Julie's hair. "I get to travel the world and never stay in one place for long. I developed my investigative skills because I'm on call every minute of the day. It was—is—the perfect job for me."

"Did you ever try to use those skills to look for your mom?" she asked cautiously.

His fingers flexed against her hair. "Yeah," Eric admitted.

"It's what got you interested in investigations in the first place, wasn't it?"

He looked down at her face, but her eyes were closed. "How did you know?"

"Just a hunch," she murmured. "Did you ever find her?"

"I tried for years, but it was all cold leads and dead ends." It was probably for the best. Any reunion would have been painful and disappointing. "I wanted my mom back, but it was clear she didn't want to be found. I gave up the search when I joined the military."

Julie snuggled deeper into his shoulder. "You are lucky to have Perry."

Eric agreed. "He didn't have a family, but he took his role as godfather very seriously. I would have taken a very different path if he hadn't been around."

"And Perry is lucky to have you in his life."

He didn't know about that. He was an inconvenience and a troublemaker, but Perry was always one step ahead of him. It had been as if he knew what Eric was going through.

"And I'm lucky, too."

Her words pierced his heart. "Why?" he asked. "I'm not perfect."

"Who wants perfect? Perfect is boring," she said as she drifted to sleep. "I'd rather have you."

THE NEXT MORNING JULIE yawned as she slipped on her stiletto heels. She smiled tiredly as she listened to Eric hum as he shaved at the bathroom sink. The man couldn't carry a tune but it sounded a little like one of the songs played last night at the club.

It was definitely a sign that they had spent too much time at the nightclub. Maybe Eric was right in insisting they take a weekend trip to Mount Rainier. She drew the curtains open and saw a clear view of snow-covered mountain.

She leaned against the glass and stared at the majestic sight. The morning sky was smudged with pink and purple. It looked quiet and peaceful. She wasn't looking for peace and she wasn't much of a nature person, but she was willing to try if it meant having Eric to herself before he returned to Washington, D.C.

"Are you sure it's a good idea to take the trip right now?" Julie called out to Eric.

"There hasn't been a good time, so let's make the time." He stepped out of the bathroom with a bath towel slung low on his hips. "I haven't seen much of this area other than the office and a few nightclubs."

"I know, but timing is important." She couldn't tear her gaze away from his sculpted chest. She licked her lips imagining how his wet skin would taste. For a moment Julie couldn't remember what she was talking about. "I need to contact the authorities about Mercedes and Tiffany."

"We can do that when we get back," he said as he walked to his closet. "There's not that much we can tell. We don't know who they're working for."

"Which is why we should stay," she murmured, and looked at the large office buildings that surrounded the hotel. The glass-and-steel structures seemed out of place with the mountain view and the manicured city parks. The architecture was aggressive and innovative. They were symbols of power and wealth that towered over the clusters of evergreen trees and the rows of up-scale shops. These businesses worked at warp speed. It was important for them to be the first in everything. The best, the biggest. She looked at the silver-and-black buildings. *The tallest.*

Technology was big business in this area. Software. Cell phones. Video games. They had to work fast because the product would be obsolete within a year or two. The companies raked in billions, although she didn't recognize any of the names. Z-Ray Studios... Boone Studios.

Boone. She tilted her head as she looked at the neon-green logo. Boone...Moon...Dune... What exactly did Boone Studios do? They were neighbors with Z-Ray, but were they also competitors?

"Julie?" Eric stood right behind her.

"Wait a second." She grabbed her cell phone from the table and did a search for Boone Studios. She tapped her toe impatiently as she waited for the results.

"What are you doing?" He tossed his clothes on the unmade bed.

"Following a hunch." A tingle swept down her spine. She had a feeling she was on to something. Julie clinked on a link and skimmed through the website. "Boone Studios also makes video games."

"I'm not surprised. Ace was telling me that gaming development is a lot like making movies. That's why they use the word *studios* in their names."

She clicked on a page on the website and gasped when she saw the biography of the owner. "No wonder I couldn't find any information on him. It's not Jeremiah Moon." She waved the phone under Eric's nose. "It's Jeremiah Boone."

"It's possible, but we don't know that for sure."

She looked at the photo that accompanied the biography. "He matches the description." Julie started to look through the photo gallery. The guy was proud of his fleet of Ferraris, his private plane and his homes.

"There are plenty of men who could match the description of slick, muscular guys who wear a lot of jewelry. We need something that connects him with Mercedes or Tiffany."

She flipped through the photo gallery and stopped at a picture of a recognizable blonde. Triumph bloomed in her chest and raced through her veins. "Something like this picture of Jeremiah Boone getting cozy with Mercedes?"

Eric stared at the picture and slowly nodded. "Yeah, something like that."

"This is great! This is perfect!" She couldn't stop smiling as she went to the camera folder on her phone. "I have all the pieces of the puzzle. I think I go to Z-Ray and...nooo!"

"What?" Eric placed a steady hand on her back. "What is it?"

"No, no, no." She stared at the screen as the frustration engulfed her. "This is not happening."

"Julie, what's wrong?"

"My pictures." Her voice wobbled as she poked at the screen. "The second one is all dark and blurry."

"The one you took inside the club?"

She pressed her lips together and nodded. "I risked everything and look! You can't see a damn thing."

13

ERIC LOOKED AT THE PHOTO on her cell phone. Julie's prized picture, the one that placed her in danger, was a complete disaster. "Don't panic," he advised.

"Too late." She flipped through the folder of photos on her phone, as if a better picture would suddenly appear. "What am I going to do now?"

"We have enough to give to Z-Ray Studios." It wasn't a slam dunk. The company's security would probably laugh them out of the office building, but at least Julie completed her goal. The possibility that she would continue without backup made his stomach twist with dread.

"They aren't going to believe us." She clenched the phone in her hands and stared at the screen. "Why should they? I'm nobody and I have no evidence."

It was true, but he didn't want her to search for more evidence. "You have a picture of the women downloading information on their cell phones."

"Big deal. It proves nothing." She tossed the phone on the table and covered her face with her hands. "I needed that picture of Mercedes and Tiffany with those programmers."

"Don't place so much importance on the pictures. You're an eyewitness."

"Not good enough," she said in a mumble as she began to pace. She looked down at the floor and bit down on her lip.

"Forget about creating another opportunity to get a picture. Mercedes and her gang are going to be more careful." He waited for her to argue but she kept pacing around the unmade bed. "Not every case is perfect. You need to work with what you have. It's all in how you present your evidence." He paused again. "You're not listening to me anymore, are you?"

She lifted her head. "I'll need a black camisole and short shorts," she declared. She glanced at the bedside clock. "It's too early to go shopping."

"What?" Why did she need that specific outfit? A memory suddenly bloomed in his mind. "Black camisole and short shorts? That's the waitress uniform at the club."

"Exactly." Julie nodded and he saw the gleam in her eyes. He recognized that look. She was becoming enthusiastic about a plan she was putting together. It was as breathtaking as it was bloodcurdling.

"You want to masquerade as a waitress? Forget it." Only Julie would come up with a gutsy move that relied on luck rather than on calculated risks. "It won't work. They'll recognize you."

"No, they won't. They didn't last night," she argued as she paced faster. He could almost feel the vibrant energy crackling from her. "I had spent the night at the bar with Lloyd and they didn't put the two aliases together."

"That was before you started taking pictures of them," Eric said as he wiped the dripping water off his face. "They're keeping an eye out for you. Even if you shaved your head, they'll remember you."

"No, this will work," she insisted, her hands up to stop his list of problems so he would listen. "Even in Agatha Christie stories, no one looks at the waiter. It's how the villain can poison the victim without being noticed."

Agatha Christie? He wasn't sure if this was any better than coming up with a strategy from one of her Sapphire books. "It doesn't work in real life."

"Do you remember what your waitress looked like last night?"

"She was five foot three, long black hair, brown eyes," he responded. "She had a tattoo of a rose on her left ankle."

Julie made a face and dropped her hands. "Okay, you're trained to notice everything. The average person won't remember."

He crossed his arms. "I'm not willing to test it out."

She blew out an exasperated sigh and placed her hands on her hips. "Then what do you recommend?"

"I suggest we stick with the original plan. Go out of town, keep our heads down and Monday morning we go to Z-Ray Studios with our information." It wasn't an aggressive plan, but the low risk was the main draw.

"Oh, Eric," she said with regret, "I want to go away with you for the weekend, but I need to finish what I started."

"You can finish it on Monday," he decided. "We're going."

Her eyes narrowed at his tone. "I'm staying."

"No, you're not." Eric ran his hand through his wet hair. He knew his demands were the wrong tactic, but the rising alarm he felt was breaking through his cool facade. He had to keep Julie hidden for the next few days if he wanted to protect her.

"Go if you want." She motioned at the majestic snow covered mountain in the distance. "You need a break before you go back to ICE. But I'm staying here. We can meet on Monday."

He tossed his hands in the air. "Why would I leave when the whole point was to get you out of town?"

"We can have a romantic getaway—" She paused. "Oh."

He didn't like the sound of that. The wobble in her voice. The disappointment.

"I'm so stupid." She slapped her palm on her forehead. "That's why you let me tie you up."

He reached for her. "Julie…"

She jerked away from him. "I thought it was an act of trust. That you trusted me and my decisions."

"I do." He trusted Julie in ways he couldn't trust his team back in D.C. But she was still a rookie on the job.

"You let me tie you up because…" Her eyes looked shiny and she blinked rapidly. "You would have done anything to keep me from leaving the hotel."

"What we did last night has nothing to do with hiding out." It was important for her to understand that. The light bondage had been an exchange of trust and power. He knew she wouldn't have tried it unless she trusted him with the dreams and desires she wasn't fully comfortable with. "I wanted you to live out your fantasy."

"No, you didn't." She took another step away and pointed accusingly at him. "You're trying to hold me back."

"I'm not. I'm trying to protect you."

She shook her head. "I can protect myself."

"No, you can't." His voice rang out.

Julie flinched as if she had been hit. "Thanks, Eric. Thanks a lot," she said bitterly. "What happened to 'you have good instincts' or 'you have raw talent'? What changed? Or was any of that true?"

"I wasn't lying." She had talent, but it wasn't enough. Not for the challenges she wanted to face.

"You don't really believe in my abilities, do you?" She strode to the table near the door and grabbed her purse. She had to get out of the hotel room. "You think I have good instincts as long as they aren't tested."

"Okay, listen." He followed her, tightening the towel that rested low on his hips. "This situation isn't the time to try out your skills."

"If you had your way it would never be the right time."

"Probably, yeah. And I have every reason to feel that way. You treat the world as if it's some amusement park. Those guys saw you interfere with their goal. They are going to hurt you."

"Not if I share the information first. Then it's a waste of time to pursue me. But unfortunately I need more pictures if I want them put away."

"So you're going to walk into the lion's den with just

a cell phone and a pair of shorts." He shook his head at the idea. "Your plan is crazy. Suicidal."

"I prefer the terms *bold* and *daring.*"

He didn't even want to consider the logistical problems of her plan. The potential drawbacks. The severe consequences if Mercedes or Tiffany recognized her. And they would.

"I'm not going to let you do this."

She tilted her head. "Seriously? You're putting your foot down? You won't *let* me?"

"That's right." He knew he was taking a big risk but he couldn't support her plan. "I won't be your backup or sidekick. In fact, I'll get in your way until you see reason and give up."

"Wow." She rubbed her forehead. "You don't know me at all."

"Julie," he said as he approached her carefully, "I'm not the enemy."

She gave a harsh bark of laughter. "You just threatened to get in my way."

"I want you to be happy." He placed his hand on her arm.

She removed his touch with a fierce shake of her arm. "No, you want to keep me fenced in."

"That's not true." He wanted her to follow her dreams and become the woman she wanted to be. But did she think she needed to face danger in order to live fully? "I want you to play it smart. Careful."

"At a distance," she added, mimicking his tone. "In full armor. Maybe put me in a plastic bubble."

"Julie, it's not like that."

"Well, I've lived like that before and I was barely existing. It was like my life was on hold." She unlatched the door and grabbed the handle. "I'm not going to live like that again."

"You don't have to, but it doesn't mean you have to be reckless."

"I want a fire burning inside me every day. I want to live outrageously." The light dimmed in her eyes. "And I'm going to do it with or without you."

"I want that for you, too."

"No, you don't." She opened the door, clearly restraining her anger, and stepped into the hallway. "You can't take me out of my cage, let me spread my wings and then think I'll go back in quietly."

"Julie, don't walk out. We're not finished."

"Yes, we are. Goodbye, Eric," she said softly and closed the door.

JULIE HURRIED AS FAST as her stiletto heels would carry her. She ducked her head as she rushed to the bank of elevators. An older man passed her in the corridor and gave her a sidelong glance. She knew it looked like she was doing a walk of shame in her black party dress and heels.

She had shared a beautiful night with Eric. She thought she had finally found someone who understood her and appreciated her strengths and weaknesses. Julie pressed her lips together as her mouth trembled. But Eric didn't think she could take care of herself. That she needed a bodyguard day and night.

She would not cry, Julie decided as she slapped the button for the elevator. Not right now. She needed to be alone and in private before the tears started to fall.

Staring at the illuminated floor numbers, she waited impatiently for the elevator. A thought she had been trying to push aside came rushing through her mind. Had Eric felt anything for her, or was she just some woman to pass the time? Did he encourage her to dream knowing the whole time she would never have a chance to act on those dreams?

Had it all been a pick-up line that she fell for?

She didn't want to think that Eric was that kind of man. He was honorable and he cared. But he didn't think much of her. She had fallen in love with a man who didn't think she was capable of crossing the street by herself.

"Come on," she muttered to herself as the elevator doors slowly opened. She stepped in and pressed a button. Crossing her arms, she stood in the corner and propped herself against the wall. She didn't feel as if she had any strength left to stand upright.

Once the elevator started to make its descent, Julie's eyes stung with tears. She would never see Eric again. Her wild fling hadn't ended the way she'd hoped. She had secretly wished Eric would have stayed in the Seattle area to be with her.

Julie shook her head at the fanciful idea. She really had to stop fantasizing. All it did was lead to heartache.

But she wouldn't stop dreaming. She wouldn't quit pursuing her dream. One day she was going to be a woman of action. She would lead the life she always wanted.

She'd show Eric. Julie's eyes narrowed as the anger bubbled inside her. She would show everyone that she could take on the world. Yes, she could be impulsive, and yes, she didn't always follow the plan. Sometimes it worked, sometimes it didn't, but she shouldn't have her world limited because she made mistakes.

It took a moment for her to see that the elevator had stopped on her floor. She walked out onto the marble mezzanine. It was quiet and empty. No one was around this early in the morning.

She studied the nightclub entrance as she headed for the sky bridge. It looked different in the day. Cold and tired. She didn't know why everyone wanted to party at that place.

Julie crossed the sky bridge, her legs heavy and slow. She didn't want to imagine what life was going to be like without Eric. She thought they were a team. Partners. The idea of going it alone wasn't as exciting.

He was more than her partner; he was her mentor. Her inspiration. She couldn't wait to embrace the day, knowing she would be with Eric. But if he couldn't support her dreams, she had to move on.

The emotions clogged her throat, threatening to suffocate her. She took a thin breath and wiped the tear from the corner of her eye. She had to stop feeling this way. Superspies didn't cry. Famous detectives didn't get emotional. They got mad, they got drunk and they shot a few people.

She didn't have that luxury, but she wasn't going to curl up in her bed for the rest of the weekend. That was the old Julie. This Julie had a job to do.

Julie entered the garage elevator and hit the button for her floor. She didn't notice anyone else was nearby until three people stepped into the elevator after her.

"What floor?" Julie asked. She glanced up when they didn't answer.

Mercedes stood in front of her. She wore the same dress as the night before. Her hair was messy and her makeup was smeared. She looked more intimidating than she did in the nightclub.

Julie didn't move. Her throat tightened and she couldn't speak. She stood frozen as the fear congealed in her stomach.

"Why don't you take your picture now," Mercedes drawled.

Julie gave a quick glance at the other two in the elevator. Would they intervene? They were both men. Big and muscular. One had a crew cut and wore jeans and T-shirt. The other was bald and wore a T-shirt and cargo pants.

"They are with me," Mercedes said with a fake smile.

Of course they were. They had an ex-military vibe about them. She never met a mercenary before but she knew one when she saw him. At another time, another place, she'd gawk and ask questions. Right now she was keeping quiet.

She looked at the alarm button near the door. It would require her to lunge for it. She'd only get one chance, but that was all she needed. Julie rocked on the balls of her feet just as Baldy blocked the button panel and pushed her away.

"Have you been waiting for me all night?" Julie asked. Eric had considered it a very real possibility, but she thought he had been paranoid.

"You shouldn't be surprised. You knew how incriminating the pictures are for me." Mercedes held out her hand. "The cell phone."

"What makes you think I didn't post the pictures online?" she asked. Let them think that it was already too late. That they should run and hide than attack.

Mercedes took a step closer and grabbed her by the hair. "You better have not," she growled in Julie's ear. "For your sake."

Okay, she made a bad call there. Julie winced as Mercedes pulled her hair. She should just give her the cell phone. She was outnumbered and out of options. The pictures weren't worth getting her ass kicked.

"Fine," she groaned. "I didn't post them."

Mercedes let go of Julie's hair and pushed her head back. "Give me the cell phone."

Julie really wanted to hit back. Pull and kick and bite. Next time, she promised herself as she opened her purse. She frowned when she didn't see her cell phone.

"It's not here." She shuffled the items in her small bag before she patted down her dress. She had no idea why she'd done that since her dress had no pockets.

Mercedes looked at the two men. "Hold her down."

"Wait!" Julie held up her hands to ward off the men. Where was her phone? She just had it. It was on the table in Eric's room. "I remember where I put it."

But was it wise to tell them the truth? Should she say it was in the room, or should she keep it far away from them? The most important picture of Mercedes returning the USB stick didn't come out, but she still had one good picture. If she lost that, she had nothing.

"Where is it?" Mercedes voice was growing higher and more impatient.

"I left it in…my car." She wanted to kick herself. The car? Bad, bad idea. Her self-defense course warned her to stay away from cars. If the bad guys tried to take her from one place to another, she was as good as dead.

Mercedes glared at her. "I don't believe you."

Great. She wasn't thinking fast enough on her feet and now she had to lie convincingly. "It's true," she insisted. Julie flinched when the elevator bell chimed. "In fact, I'll take you there right now."

"Why are you being so cooperative all of a sudden?"

Yeah, that did seem suspicious. She was trying to lie and think several steps ahead while her mind was racing as fast as her pulse. "Do you want the phone or not?" she asked.

Mercedes motioned for her to exit the elevator. "Lead the way."

She should have said it was in the hotel room, Julie decided as she walked down the ramp to her car with the two men flanking her. But she didn't have a hotel key. She needed to figure a way to get into her car and create a barrier between her and the bad guys.

"What kind of car?" Mercedes asked.

"It's the light blue MINI Cooper. Right there in the corner." Eric had been right. It really was a bad idea parking there. There was no security camera coverage or emergency call button. If she got out of this unscathed, she would always find the safest parking spot from now on. Hell, she would splurge for valet parking.

Julie looked around the parking structure. It was deserted on a Saturday morning. Too early for the shops to be opened. If she screamed for help, would anyone hear? If she kicked off her shoes and ran, would she get far?

She reached inside her purse. Crew Cut grabbed her upper arm and wrenched it behind her back. Julie gasped in pain.

"No sudden moves," Crew Cut warned her.

Her eyes watered from the sharp shooting pain. "I was just getting my keys. I swear."

Crew Cut waited for Mercedes's nod before he let her go.

"That's going to leave a bruise." Julie rubbed her arm. "My God, you guys are suspicious." She pushed the button on her key. Her heart was beating wildly, the need to flee rushing through her bloodstream, as she placed her hand on the handle.

"Stop." Mercedes pulled Julie away from the car. "Tyler will look."

"Tyler?" Crew Cut's name was Tyler? Oh, that was so disappointing. She expected a nickname like Spike or Bruiser.

She cringed as the man sat in the driver's seat. He was too big to sit straight in her car. She watched with growing dread as he rifled through the discarded coffee cups and candy wrappers.

"Uh…sorry about the mess." How was she going to get out of this one? She gripped her car key in her hand. She'd use it as a blade if she had to defend herself.

Tyler looked around the console and in the glove compartment. "I don't see a phone."

"It's gotta be in there. Keep looking." She glanced over her shoulder, hoping to find an emergency exit sign. "You can't miss it. It's bright pink."

Tyler ignored her and looked at Mercedes. "No phone."

"Here, let me look." She just needed to get in the car, lock the door and drive full speed ahead. Maybe swerve a little so she could run over Mercedes's Louboutins.

"I don't think so," Tyler said as he got out of her car.

"Maybe I should call it." Her eyes widened as she considered the idea. She'd call Eric. They may have just had an argument, but he'd drop everything to help her. She knew it deep in her bones. "I always have to do that when I put down my phone."

Mercedes glared at her. "You are getting on my nerves. Stop talking."

"You want the phone," she reminded her.

"I'm not falling for it. You and I both know you'd call that hottie you're working with."

Damn. Mercedes obviously read the same books.

"Julie!" Eric's voice echoed in the parking garage. Julie whirled around and saw him running toward them. He was shirtless, barefoot and wearing a faded pair of jeans.

Eric's presence was all the distraction she needed. As Tyler went to block Eric, Julie turned and swiped the metal key across Baldy's face. He let go of her arm and howled, clutching his face. She pushed him with all her might and lurched for the open car door.

She scrambled into the seat and was about to slam the door when Mercedes blocked her. Julie clawed and kicked. Mercedes took the blows as she pressed something cold and metallic against Julie's neck.

"Sweet dreams," Mercedes said with a wicked laugh.

Julie heard a crackle of electricity. She went rigid as the pain coursed through her body before everything went dark.

14

JULIE WOKE UP WITH A START. Her heart leaped against her chest, her throat squeezed tight and her muscles locked as if under attack. She noticed three things: she was not in the parking garage, she was lying on thick beige carpeting and she felt as if she'd been run over a few times.

She groaned and gingerly touched her neck. Mercedes must have used a Taser. There was no wound or burn yet the electric charge had been enough to make her drop.

Julie slowly sat up and noticed the room she was in. It was designed to impress and intimidate, from the big expensive desk to the bookshelf that had very few books but plenty of awards. Weird art hung on the walls that only a twisted soul could appreciate. Then again, she might be a little judgmental about someone who would use a Taser and then dump her on the floor.

She slowly turned and gasped when she saw Eric sprawled on the floor. He was a few feet away but she could see the bruises on his chest and abdomen. A small cut bled on his forehead and there was a swelling on his cheek. "What happened to you?" she asked as she crawled over to him. "I swear, that Mercedes is going down."

"By you?" He winced and held his arm at the elbow. "You suck at self-defense."

"I am so sorry this happened to you." Julie placed her hand on his forehead and looked into his eyes. She could tell that he was in pain. "Let me help you up."

"Seriously, you should get your money back on that self-defense course." He grimaced as she assisted him into a sitting position.

"I drew blood on one of them," Julie reminded him as she took the edge of her skirt and pressed it on his bleeding knuckles. She noticed that he didn't pull away and couldn't tell if that was a good or a bad sign. "Give me a Taser and I could have done some permanent damage."

"Don't be too sure about that," he muttered. "You probably wouldn't know how to work it."

"Oh, now that's just mean." She clucked her tongue as she silently catalogued his injuries. "And this from a guy who came out of the fight bloodied and captured."

He gently touched the swelling on his cheek with his fingertips. "You should have seen the other guy."

Julie rolled her eyes. "Yeah, right."

"No, really," a female voice said at the far end of the room. Julie turned and saw Mercedes at the door. Damn, she should have known they wouldn't have left them unattended.

Julie saw the Taser in Mercedes's manicured hands. Her stomach curled as she remembered the jolt of intense pain. She was tempted to rush and attack the blonde, but the sight of the weapon made her hesitate.

"Tyler is all messed up," Mercedes complained. "Your boyfriend here just about took his head off."

Julie glanced at Eric for confirmation. He gave her an I-told-you-so look. "Damn, I miss everything!" she said with a grumble. She would have loved to see Eric in action.

"You're bleeding all over the carpet," Julie said to Eric and held his jaw as she studied the cut on his forehead. "Where are we?" she whispered.

He tried to shrug but had to stop halfway. He winced and wrapped an arm around her bruised ribs. "Not far from the hotel."

"Stop talking," Mercedes ordered and patted the Taser. "I don't trust you two."

"With good reason," Julie said out of the corner of her mouth. She stood up and wobbled on her stilettos as she took a peek out the windows. She saw Mount Rainier and it was a very similar view from the one at the hotel.

Julie faced Mercedes. "Are we at Boone Studios?"

Mercedes's eyes widened in surprise and she tilted her face as if she sensed trouble. She didn't answer and Julie decided that was enough of a confirmation.

"How did you come up with that?" Eric asked.

"I can observe and deduce," she told him. "I can also add and subtract."

Eric groaned, lay back down on the floor and closed his eyes. "Are we going to do this again? Do you really think this is the time and place?"

"Long division is still a challenge," she said as if he

hadn't spoken, "but I can do the math. I can tell that Jeremiah Boone is going to meet us shortly."

"Huh," Mercedes said and gave Julie a speculative look. "You're kind of smart for a party girl."

Party girl? Where the hell did she get that idea? Julie knew she looked messed up, but not as if she'd been doing men and drugs all night.

She saw Eric slowly open his eyes and they shared a brief look. He didn't have to say anything or give a signal. She was on the same wavelength as Eric.

Okay, she could do that. Party Girl Julie coming up. She wore the wrong dress and didn't have the makeup for it, but this was a special circumstance.

She tried to make her eyes look bleary as she tousled her hair. "Mercedes, I am very smart. You should see me when I'm not wasted."

Mercedes stood to attention. "How do you know my name?" she asked sharply.

Right. Julie tried to look as if she were in a drug-induced fog. She needed to be more careful on sharing what she knew. "It doesn't matter." She staggered to a chair in front of the desk and half fell, half slid into the seat. "I need a Vicodin. I have this mother of a hangover."

"That's from the Taser."

She stilled at the unfamiliar male voice. The tension in the room thickened as Jeremiah Boone walked into the room. Julie tossed her hair, allowing it to fall in her face, as she studied the man.

Flashy. That was her first impression of him. His gray suit was tailored to exaggerate his shoulders. His scruffy beard and slicked-back hair were a little too carefully maintained. His bright gold jewelry distracted her. It was blinding as it hung from his ear, neck and wrist. She saw the gold on his hands and the jewelry looked more like brass knuckles than rings.

Appearances definitely mattered to Jeremiah Boone. In his office, in his clothes and in his women. She flicked a look at Mercedes, who stayed at the door.

But Jeremiah was taken in with the appearance of his other guest. He barely gave her a look. His attention was on Eric. Eric might be bloodied and lying on the floor, but Jeremiah saw him as the threat.

She might be able to use it to her advantage. She needed to distract Jeremiah so Eric could take them by surprise. If he *could* attack? She speculated, noticing Eric's slow and painful movements.

"I could use a drink," she declared and leaned back in her chair to spread out her legs. "Have any beer?"

"It's the morning," Mercedes said in a withering tone.

Julie tossed her hand in the air as if the time of day didn't matter. "A Bloody Mary, then? How about a mimosa?"

"I want the cell phone." Jeremiah's deep voice cut through her request. He sat down at his desk and waited for Eric to respond.

Eric sat up and Mercedes took a few steps, her weapon aimed at him. Jeremiah had remained seated, but she saw how his body reacted. They were watching Eric very closely.

It was up to her to attack.

Julie stood up and stretched. Her movements were loose as she cupped her breasts before reaching over her head. She tilted her head back and gave an earthy moan. She felt everyone's eyes on her.

"I swear, it's too early in the morning for this," she announced, trying to slur her words. "Jeremiah, dude, let's cut a deal."

"Julie, what are you doing?" Eric's words held a bite of warning.

She shushed him before she hooked her finger in her mouth and looked at Jeremiah. "I want to work for you. I want to do what Mercedes and Tiffany do for you."

Jeremiah tilted his head, his earring catching the morning light. "How do you know their names?"

"I'm a regular at the nightclub. But I can't afford Versace and Louboutin," she said with a pout. "Not on my salary."

"You don't know anything about my girls," he said, dismissing her claim as he watched Eric through hooded eyes.

"I know that they target computer programmers from Z-Ray," she said, pleased at how her words gave him a start. "They get real friendly with the guys so they can lift their keys. Then they excuse themselves to the restroom and download the information from their USB sticks to their phones. They return the keys without any of the men knowing."

Jeremiah silently glared at Mercedes.

The blonde held up her hands in protest. "I don't know how she found out."

Julie looked down and made a show of readjusting her halter. "Dude, if I know what Mercedes and Tiffany do, other people know, too." She pushed her breasts together and jiggled them with her hands. "It's only a matter of time before the geeks wise up."

"I don't need to hire another girl," Jeremiah said as he watched Julie's hands.

"You don't have to," she said as she walked to his desk, her hips rocking side to side. Julie saw Jeremiah staring at her legs. His tongue darted past his lips as he saw her shoes. "All you have to do is replace Mercedes with me."

"What?" Mercedes's voice shook with outrage and she motioned at Julie with her Taser. "Don't listen to her!"

"Mercedes's gotten sloppy. They both have," Julie told him, trying to ignore the weapon. "The other night Tiffany forgot her cable to download information. They almost got caught."

Mercedes stomped her foot. "That's an exaggeration."

"But there is some truth to it?" Jeremiah asked, his tone quelling Mercedes's defense.

"And I was able to get several pictures of them," she confided. "It's time to upgrade. Let them go."

"Upgrade?" Mercedes said in a hiss. "Why you—"

Jeremiah held up his hand to stop Mercedes. Julie didn't like riling someone with a Taser, or having her back to the unpredictable woman. But she knew that Mercedes was being ruled by her emotions. She wasn't thinking or watching. She was reacting.

"Those pictures are going to eventually lead back to you. It's how I found you." She sat on the edge of the desk, allowing her dress to hike up high. If the glittering of his eyes was any indication, Jeremiah was enjoying the view.

"All this for Mercedes's job?" he asked.

"What can I say? I have champagne taste." She leaned forward, letting Jeremiah get a good look at her breasts. It made her skin crawl, but she tried not to show it. "I want everything life has to offer, but I don't want to work that hard."

"A girl like you shouldn't have to," Jeremiah murmured as he placed his hand on her bare thigh.

Julie didn't flinch. Instead, she smiled in response and she had a spurt of pleasure when she heard Mercedes's jealous growl. Julie straightened and let her foot sway gently. Just as she expected, Jeremiah's attention was drawn to her legs.

"And I'm happy to give you the pictures in exchange," Julie said casually. "Even better, I can delete them."

"You haven't shared them with anyone else?" he asked mildly.

"Julie…"

She heard Eric's warning, but she was already aware of the trap. If she didn't play this right, she was going to wind up in a hospital or in a hearse.

"Stop calling me Julie," she said to Eric over her shoulder. "I'm not going by that name anymore." She flattened her hands on the desk and leaned back. It made her open and vulnerable to Jeremiah and her nerves were shredded. "I think I'm going to go by Sapphire."

Eric groaned. She couldn't tell if he understood her

signal. She was about to make her move and go all Sapphire on Jeremiah.

"Sapphire," Mercedes said with a snort.

"Tell me, Sapphire…" Jeremiah rose from his seat and placed his hands on either side of her. He towered above her, trapping her on the desk. "Did you share the pictures with anyone else?"

She smiled but her stomach roiled. She needed him closer, but she couldn't take it anymore. Julie curled her hand into a fist and punched him hard in the nose.

She saw the spurt of blood as he howled. Jeremiah staggered back and covered his nose with his hands. Just as she had hoped. Julie took advantage of his exposed position and kicked him in the groin with her pointed heels.

As Jeremiah doubled over, she sensed that Mercedes was rushing to attack. Julie jumped off the desk and slammed her stiletto heel on Jeremiah's foot.

The man crumpled to the ground. She whirled around to take on Mercedes, but she wasn't behind her. She was trapped in Eric's headlock. Julie raised her fists above her head and did a little victory dance.

"Where did you get that move?" Eric asked as he struggled to keep Mercedes still.

"I got an A in my self-defense class," she said proudly. She sounded out of breath and the adrenaline was rushing so fast in her body she felt a little lightheaded. "I told you my shoes were my secret weapon."

"I can't believe you did that," Eric called out as he kept Mercedes from grabbing the Taser on the floor. "Boone is twice your size."

"Excuse me?" Julie was offended. "Try three times as big. *At least.*"

He tightened his grip on Mercedes as she squirmed and kicked. "Don't forget to—"

"Frisk and immobilize him. I know." She watched Mercedes fight back. If Eric didn't watch out, the blonde was going to sink her teeth into his arm. "Need help with that one?"

"I think I can manage."

Julie walked over and picked up the Taser. She pushed the button and exclaimed with excitement when it crackled. "Can I at least use this on her?"

"What?" Mercedes yelled.

"No," Eric said firmly. "I don't let you use a gun. Do you really think I'm going to let you play with electric voltage?"

"She used it on me," Julie reminded him as she twirled the gun with her trigger finger. "Fair is fair."

"Don't you dare!" Mercedes tried to get away from her.

Julie pointed the Taser at the blonde. "Then lie on your stomach. Keep your hands where I can see them."

Mercedes reluctantly followed her orders, cursing under her breath.

"And no talking," Julie added. She gave a quick look at Eric. "What do you think of my skills now?"

"Keep swinging that thing around and you're going to Taser yourself," he said.

"Funny." She saw Eric frown. She wanted to rush over and comfort him, but she knew he was too proud and would decline her offer. "I'm going to tie up Boone and Mercedes. You can call the police."

He cradled his arm and gritted his teeth. "Why do you get to have all the fun?"

"Because you're the sidekick." And because he was in no condition to help. Not that she would tell him that.

"Now I'm back to being a sidekick?"

She saw a sneaky movement from the corner of her eye. She immediately pointed the Taser at Mercedes. "I'm really looking for a reason to use this."

Mercedes sagged against the floor and surrendered.

"I really need to get me one of these," Julie told Eric.

He groaned. "God help us all."

TWO DAYS LATER JULIE strode into the offices of Gunthrie Security & Investigations. She felt like a different person. Bolder. Stronger. She showed that she could take care of herself—and her sidekick—when the occasion called for it. More important, she proved it to herself.

She walked to her cubicle and stared at the jumble of uniforms. Her sunny attitude took a dip. She may have helped uncover an act of corporate espionage, but her job description hadn't changed.

As much as she adored Perry and enjoyed working with her colleagues, she didn't think she could keep being Uniform Girl. She wanted action and adventure and that meant leaving the cubicle. If it meant she would have to find work elsewhere, she would. It wouldn't be easy, but she was ready to move on.

Though there were some things from which she couldn't move on. Julie glanced at Eric's office and saw the door was closed. She wasn't sure if she should go and knock. He had been guarded, very aloof, after they had called the police.

At first she thought it was because he was trying to stay strong when he was in so much pain. But she hadn't heard from him since they'd given statements. Her call went unanswered and none of the excuses she came up for him erased her uneasiness.

"Oh, hi, Julie." Asia looked up from an opened file and stopped at her cubicle. "Perry's called a meeting."

"This early in the morning?" She looked around and noticed everyone else was walking into the conference room. Julie dropped her purse in the bottom drawer of her desk as Asia waited for her. "So…" Julie tried to hide her smile. "How was your weekend?"

"Not as exciting as yours." Asia playfully swatted her with the file folder.

"Oh, you heard?" she asked modestly. "Gossip travels fast around here."

Asia linked her arm with Julie's. "I'm sorry I didn't believe you," she said. "I really thought…"

"It's okay, Asia." She patted her friend's hand. "You were right to question it."

"I should have believed you," she said as she shook her head with regret. "I should have been there to back you up!"

"Next time," Julie promised. She opened the door to the conference room and stumbled to a halt at the threshold as she was greeted with confetti and cheers from her coworkers.

Julie spluttered the confetti out of her mouth as she stared at the banner and balloons. "What's all this?" she asked.

"Julie!" Perry greeted her with a big hug. "Thanks

to you, we have a very lucrative security contract with Z-Ray Studios."

"How? Why?" She didn't expect anything like this. She didn't look that far ahead and had only wanted to figure out what had been going on.

"Z-Ray is very appreciative and Eric finalized the deal last night," Perry explained.

"That's great." Her heart did a funny flip at the mention of Eric. She looked around the crowded room but didn't see him.

"And," Perry continued, "because you saved our bacon with your perseverance and instinct, you are moving out of your cubicle and moving into Eric's old office."

"Old office?"

Perry nodded. "You can move in right away. Eric's medical leave is over and he returned to D.C. late last night."

"He left?" Her heart stopped. No, he wouldn't do that without saying goodbye. Without promising to keep in touch. Not after all they'd been through. Not when they had shared something special.

Perry turned to the group. "Let's get the guest of honor some coffee cake."

"Eric left?" she repeated weakly.

"That reminds me…" Perry snapped his fingers and reached into his pocket. He pulled out an inner-office envelope. "Eric says congratulations and he wanted me to give you this."

She grabbed the brown envelope from Perry's hands and clutched it to her chest. She had no idea what was inside, or what he wrote. Her heart was galloping as she made her way to a corner and cautiously opened the heavy envelope.

> Julie—forget everything I said that morning. You will make a great detective. I'm glad we're on the same side.
> E

She tipped the contents into her hands. Her cell phone slid out along with a gold cigarette lighter and Swiss Army knife.

Julie bit her lip as she stared at the gift. He remembered her joke about how a detective only needed a cell phone, lighter and pocketknife. It should make her smile but she was breaking inside.

Because she knew what he was saying with the gift. She would be fine on her own. He didn't need to watch over her anymore.

It was what she'd always wanted. His respect. His belief in her abilities. But it wasn't enough. She was greedy. She wanted the whole dream.

15

Two months later

JULIE FLINCHED WHEN SHE heard the ball crashing against the pins. She looked up just as Asia exclaimed with joy and punched her fists high in the air. The electronic beep and whoops of the overhead monitor declared a strike.

So that was what a strike sounded like. Julie yawned and drank the last of her warm soda. She never did like bowling.

"Congratulations," Julie said as she discreetly removed the earpiece and slipped it inside her purse. "Looks like you won. Again."

"I wonder how high I could really score," her friend said as she looked at the scoreboard. "It was so tempting to let the ball fly tonight."

"That would have ruined our decoy assignment. Those guys would have been too intimidated to talk to us. You know, that's why I threw only gutter balls."

"Oh, is that why?" Asia said in a teasing tone. "That

was so great of you for swallowing your pride and taking one for the team."

"Just do me a favor and erase my bowling score from the video feed. I don't want to see that showing up during the highlight reel at the next Christmas party."

Asia smiled. "I'll see what I can do."

Julie stretched and rubbed her hand against her back. She had spent the past few hours bowling and flirting with a bunch of suspected cheaters. "I can't believe I'm saying this, but I miss the nightclub."

Asia patted Julie's arm. "That nightclub is so boring. It's the same people dancing to the same songs and giving the same pick-up lines."

"Maybe." She bent down to take off her rented shoes. "But at least I get to wear stilettos at the nightclub."

"That's true. And who knew those bowling shoes were so dangerous. When you slipped, I thought you were going to slide down that alley. You recovered well."

"Thank you."

"I kept scuffing the soles of my shoes after that. But don't I look cute? What do you think of Bowling Asia?" She raised her arms and twirled like a model on the runway.

"Adorable. Only you could rock that shade of yellow." Her friend wore baggy jeans and an oversized bowling shirt that hid their brand-new video feed, but it couldn't diminish her glamour. The bowlers on the other lane, including Julie's target, had been showing off to catch Asia's attention.

"We should pair up again," Asia said as she gathered

her shoes from under the plastic chair. "I forgot how fun it was to be out in the field."

"I'm all for it." It was different and had its own challenges, but she liked it. She and Asia worked in tandem, but she missed working with Eric.

Eric. She needed to stop thinking about him. He had never called or emailed. Their fling was officially over.

"Everyone is meeting up at the pizza place across the parking lot," Asia said. "Come celebrate with us."

She'd rather curl up in bed and pull the covers over her head. "Thanks, but I'm not really in the mood."

"Julie, I insist. You did a super job as a decoy. Because of you, we got some great video of Wade cheating on his girlfriend."

"Wade would have stuck his tongue down any woman's throat. It just happened to be mine." She shuddered from the memory. Either decoying was getting easier or their targets were getting slimier.

"I thought he was a creep even before he offered you money for sex," Asia confided as they walked to the main desk with their rental shoes.

"Can you imagine what he would have pulled if I had worn my Trashy Julie alias? You would have had to use your kung fu on him."

"With pleasure." She placed the shoes on the counter and looked at Julie's white T-shirt, faded jeans and knee-high boots. "Which alias are you?"

"No alias." She didn't feel as if she needed to hide under a sexy disguise. "It's just me."

"I approve," Asia said with a smile. "You'll have to let me wear those boots for my date tomorrow."

Asia wanted to borrow her clothes? That surprised

Julie. Maybe she had kept some elements of her sexy aliases in her everyday clothes. "Sure, but I don't think we're the same size."

"I'll squeeze into them." Asia slung her arm over Julie's shoulder as they walked by the arcade. "Now tell me the truth. You're not getting bored with decoying, are you?"

"No." She should have realized that her general lack of enthusiasm was becoming noticeable. "I don't want to do it forever, but I like having a chance to brush up my skills."

"Is there anything else that's bothering you?"

"The guys I meet in the line of work are awful." She couldn't stop comparing the men to how great Eric had been with her. "I really want to call up Wade's girlfriend and tell her to get out now."

"She'll make that decision once she sees these pictures." Asia patted the button of her shirt that was the video feed.

"And I can't help think how great I had it with Eric," Julie confessed as they walked out of the bowling alley. "I should make up an excuse to contact him. What do you think?"

"Forget about him," Asia said bluntly. "If he hasn't contacted you by now, he never will."

Julie stopped in the middle of the parking lot. That wasn't the advice she wanted to hear. "Didn't you once tell me to stop fantasizing and go for it?"

"You had a wonderful time with Eric, but it was never meant to be permanent. It ran its course. You shouldn't concentrate on the fact that it's over. Celebrate the fact that it happened."

That sounded oddly familiar. "Are you quoting Dr. Seuss?"

"Paraphrasing," Asia said with a guilty smile. "But the guy is wise."

Maybe one day she would remember Eric without the pain and misery. Right now it hurt just thinking about him and what she had lost.

"If you're feeling social, come by for a slice," Asia said as she headed for the pizzeria. "The peppers they use are so hot it will wipe out the taste of Wade."

Julie made a face and stuck out her tongue as if it was contaminated. "Nights like these make me wish I got to work on the security contract for Z-Ray."

"You'll get there," Asia said and waved goodbye.

Julie gave a small smile as she walked over to her car, which was parked directly under a light and in plain view of the bowling alley entrance. One day she would get to work on a prestigious contract. With a little patience and a lot of studying, she'll have her dream job.

Julie pulled her keys from her purse and reached her MINI Cooper when a shadow fell upon her. Her heart lurched and instincts kicked in. Julie whirled around on her heel and struck out her arm. Her fist collided with a large hand. She tried to pull back but her assailant grabbed her wrist and immobilized her with little effort.

"You're getting better."

Eric? She stared at him as the call to fight seeped from her body. She must be hallucinating. He seemed taller. Leaner. And, damn it, sexier.

He let go of her wrist and slid his hands into his pockets. "Now what is a nice girl like you doing in a place like this?"

ERIC SAW JULIE'S EYES narrow before she crossed her arms and braced her legs. She wasn't happy to see him. At least she didn't try to throw another punch.

He didn't blame her for being angry. He had tried to be honorable, but that bit him in the ass. Typical. He had been in the wrong and hoped it wasn't too late to correct his mistakes.

Julie's gaze went from his head to his feet. "Where's a Taser gun when you need one?"

Eric raised his eyebrows. "No need to get violent."

"Bowling does that to me," she said, clenching her hands at her side.

"I thought you were on a decoy assignment."

"I was. We just finished and everyone is at the pizzeria. Why don't you go over and say hello to them?"

"Maybe later." He didn't want to be with anyone else. He wanted Julie.

She had haunted his dreams until he couldn't sleep. He missed her warmth and generous spirit. He wanted to be surprised by her crazy plans and be part of her world.

Julie didn't look lovesick and wasn't wasting away. From what Perry had said in emails, Julie had developed into a strong and confident woman. Eric studied the fitted T-shirt and snug jeans. "No alias tonight?"

"No," she replied sharply. "How did you know?"

"Because I know you well. I can see you through the aliases. To the real you." He saw her guarded expression and knew it was time to shut up.

"What are you doing here, Eric?"

He decided to play it casual since Julie wasn't thrilled to see him. He hadn't expected her to throw her arms around him…. No, that wasn't true. He had hoped for an enthusiastic welcome. He should have known better. It'd been two long months.

"I was here to discuss the Jeremiah Boone case with the lawyers," he said. "I decided to check up on Perry, as well. He told me where you were."

"And you might as well see how I'm doing since you were in the neighborhood?" Her nostrils flared as she reined in her anger. "No need. I'm doing fine. Better than fine."

"So I hear. You're training to become a private investigator." It wasn't right to feel proud. He had nothing to do with it, but he was pleased that the incident with Jeremiah Boone didn't prevent Julie from focusing on her dreams.

"That's right. I'm working toward a license."

He smiled. "And what's this about being the star pupil in self-defense?"

Julie shrugged. "I don't know what you're talking about. You said yourself that I suck at self-defense."

His smile faded. "I told you to forget everything I said that day." He had tried to keep her away from a dangerous situation, but instead, he had said things that could have permanently crushed her spirit.

"You didn't tell me. You wrote a letter that explained nothing." She glared at him. "I never took you for a coward."

This reunion wasn't going as planned. Eric nervously rubbed the back of his neck. "I had to return to D.C. and was immediately thrown into handling a crisis."

"That is not a good excuse." She pointed at him with

an accusing finger. "You could have at least tried to contact me."

"Okay, I couldn't face you," he admitted rawly. "How could I, knowing that I fell short in your eyes?"

Her jaw dropped. "That's not true. Who told you that? Whoever they were, they lied."

"No one had to tell me. You were always looking at me as if I'm a hero." He lowered his gaze in shame. "I wanted to be your hero, but I failed to protect you in Boone's office."

"You protected me," Julie argued. "You were injured and hurting, but you tackled that crazy woman with a Taser gun."

"It never should have escalated like that." He thrust his fingers in his hair as he remembered that moment in the parking lot. Pure terror had flooded his heart when he had seen Julie collapse to the ground. "Your safety had been at risk because of my error of judgment."

"Is that why you left without saying goodbye? Because you thought I was disappointed in you?"

"It wasn't until we were giving our statements to the police. As I was telling them what happened, I realized I was an obstacle for you. I was blocking you from living out your dreams. You don't need to put up with that. And my leaving was the best thing for you."

"How do you figure that?"

"You now work in a very supportive environment. Perry listens to your ideas. Your coworkers admire your skills and they will do anything to help you."

"I had that with you, too." She took a step forward. "You didn't agree with me on everything, but that was a good thing. I didn't need a yes-man or a groupie. I needed a partner."

"You don't need me now." It hurt to say it. He once thought Julie couldn't do anything without him, but she'd proved him wrong every step of the way. "You accomplished everything by yourself. You hunted for crucial information and you put the puzzle together. I couldn't help you when you faced Jeremiah."

"So you weren't at the top of your game that day. It happens." She reached out and touched his arm. "You shouldn't throw away a partnership because of one bad day."

"Is that what we had? A partnership?"

"You didn't see me as a partner." She dropped her hand. "You saw me as your protégée or your responsibility."

"You're right, I did. I should have seen what we really were—a couple."

"We were never a couple," she said flippantly. "I was Batman and you were Robin."

"I'm serious, Julie." He placed his hand on her shoulder. "Tell me the truth. Are you still in love with me?"

She looked away. "After how you left me? What do you think?"

"I think you are." He hoped and prayed that she was. "You're not one who would easily fall out of love."

She tried to shrug off his hand. "You sound very arrogant."

"I wanted to be a hero in your eyes," he confessed.

"You are, Eric," she said quietly and faced him. "But not in the ways that you think. I'm not expecting you to cheat death or sacrifice your freedom to be a hero."

"What do you think is a hero?"

"It's in the way you take care of those around you. Like…" She gestured with her hands as she tried to explain. "Like how you let everyone have their moment in the sun."

"That's not heroic."

"It is to us. You took care of us as if we were your family. You took the time to teach us the skills we needed, even though it wasn't in your job description. You always looked after us."

"I thought you found my protective nature suffocating."

"I did sometimes. But the reason you are my hero is because your heart was in the right place. Even when I was messing up and didn't have any experience to fall back on, you still supported my dream of becoming a private eye."

He cradled her face in his hands. "I tried to stay away. I thought it was for the best, but I missed you."

"Good," she said. "I'm glad to hear I'm not the only one who suffered."

"I quit my job," he revealed as he caressed her cheeks with his fingers.

She stiffened in his hold. "Why the hell did you do that?"

"I'm moving here. For good." Eric watched her expression. She didn't look happy. Julie looked confused and distrustful.

"To help Perry?" she asked cautiously.

"No, I'm here because you're here." He pressed his forehead against hers and closed his eyes. "I'm in love with you and I want to share my life with you."

His heart ached as time stood still. Was she going to accept his love, or would she push him away?

"You're going to regret it," she whispered. "You'll get bored with the job. With me."

He looked into her eyes. "Never," he promised. "You are the most exciting thing that has ever happened to me."

She tilted her head away. "I seriously doubt that."

"Then I'll show you every day how much you excite me. I want to wake up with you every morning and hold you in my arms every night."

"Go on."

"I want you at my side at work. I'll request that we work as partners. Equal partners."

"Are you sure you want to do that? You are a former special agent. You spent your whole career fighting crime. I spent mine folding uniforms."

"We're bringing our strengths and weaknesses to the table. Your instincts and my experience. Your enthusiasm will balance out my caution."

"We make a good team," she said, warming up to the idea. "But before you get any crazy notions, I want you to know that I'm not giving back the office. It's mine now, fair and square."

"We could share. We're partners, after all," he said, gathering her close. He didn't want to take that office from Julie. She'd hated her cubicle and the workspace represented her hard-won success. But he couldn't resist teasing her.

"No, but nice try."

"Yeah, that wouldn't be a good idea," he agreed as he brushed his mouth against her forehead and swept his lips against her closed eyes. "We'd never get any work done."

"You are going to have to earn that office," she warned him, her voice breathless. "In the meantime, no one is working at my old cubicle."

"I could always move into the supply closet," he mused as he grazed his mouth against her cheekbones. "You can visit me anytime you want."

"I just might accept your invitation." She grasped his jaw with her hands and kissed him.

Eric tried to show an ounce of self-control, but he had been dreaming about her kisses for weeks. As soon as her lips brushed against his, his restraint snapped. He held Julie tight against him and deepened the kiss.

She tasted just as he remembered. Her soft lips yielded as he invaded her mouth. Julie caught his tongue and drew him in. She speared her fingers into his hair and held him tightly as she kissed him fiercely.

He needed this. He needed her sweet, hot kisses. He was starved for her touch and her affection. He was insatiable for Julie. He had been in danger of not feeling, not caring anymore, but Julie had changed that. She was his muse and inspiration. He may never be the hero she deserved, but he would be the man she needed at her side.

Julie tore away and pressed her swollen lips together. "Come on, Eric, let's get out of here."

She laced her fingers through his. Her hand was small and delicate, but he felt her strength. He loved everything about this woman, and he knew he could rely on her. No matter what they faced, Julie would have his back.

And Julie knew he would do the same for her. She didn't have to ask. He would be there.

Eric raised her hand and kissed her fingers. "Where are we going?" he asked.

"Home," she said simply.

Home. He was going home with Julie. His partner, his love, his life. Eric held her hand tighter. "Lead the way."

* * * * *

PASSION

COMING NEXT MONTH
AVAILABLE JUNE 26, 2012

#693 LEAD ME HOME
Sons of Chance
Vicki Lewis Thompson
Matthew Tredway has made a name for himself as a world-class horse trainer. Only, after one night with Aurelia Smith, he's the one being led around by the nose....

#694 THE GUY MOST LIKELY TO...
A Blazing Hot Summer Read
Leslie Kelly, Janelle Denison and Julie Leto
Every school has one. That special guy, the one every girl had to have or they'd just die! Did you ever wonder what happened to him? Come back to school with three of Blaze's bestselling authors and find out how great the nights are after the glory days are over....

#695 TALL, DARK & RECKLESS
Heather MacAllister
After interviewing a thousand men, dating coach Piper Scott knows handsome daredevil foreign journalist Mark Banning is definitely not her type—but what if he's her perfect man?

#696 NO HOLDS BARRED
Forbidden Fantasies
Cara Summers
Defense attorney Piper MacPherson is being threatened by a stalker and protected by FBI profiler Duncan Sutherland. Her problem? She's not sure which is more dangerous....

#697 BREATHLESS ON THE BEACH
Flirting with Justice
Wendy Etherington
When PR exec Victoria Holmes attends a client's beach-house party, she has no idea there'll be cowboys—well, one cowboy. Lucky for Victoria, Jarred McKenna's not afraid to get a little wet....

#698 NO GOING BACK
Uniformly Hot!
Karen Foley
Army Special Ops commando Chase Rawlins has been trained to handle anything. Only, little does he guess how much he'll enjoy "handling" sexy publicist Kate Fitzgerald!

You can find more information on upcoming Harlequin® titles, free excerpts and more at www.Harlequin.com.

REQUEST YOUR FREE BOOKS!
2 FREE NOVELS PLUS 2 FREE GIFTS!

◆ Harlequin® *Blaze*™

red-hot reads!

YES! Please send me 2 FREE Harlequin® Blaze™ novels and my 2 FREE gifts (gifts are worth about $10). After receiving them, if I don't wish to receive any more books, I can return the shipping statement marked "cancel." If I don't cancel, I will receive 6 brand-new novels every month and be billed just $4.49 per book in the U.S. or $4.96 per book in Canada. That's a saving of at least 14% off the cover price. It's quite a bargain. Shipping and handling is just 50¢ per book in the U.S. and 75¢ per book in Canada.* I understand that accepting the 2 free books and gifts places me under no obligation to buy anything. I can always return a shipment and cancel at any time. Even if I never buy another book, the two free books and gifts are mine to keep forever.

151/351 HDN FEQE

Name	(PLEASE PRINT)	

Address		Apt. #

City	State/Prov.	Zip/Postal Code

Signature (if under 18, a parent or guardian must sign)

Mail to the **Reader Service:**
IN U.S.A.: P.O. Box 1867, Buffalo, NY 14240-1867
IN CANADA: P.O. Box 609, Fort Erie, Ontario L2A 5X3

Not valid for current subscribers to Harlequin Blaze books.

Want to try two free books from another line?
Call 1-800-873-8635 or visit www.ReaderService.com.

* Terms and prices subject to change without notice. Prices do not include applicable taxes. Sales tax applicable in N.Y. Canadian residents will be charged applicable taxes. Offer not valid in Quebec. This offer is limited to one order per household. All orders subject to credit approval. Credit or debit balances in a customer's account(s) may be offset by any other outstanding balance owed by or to the customer. Please allow 4 to 6 weeks for delivery. Offer available while quantities last.

Your Privacy—The Reader Service is committed to protecting your privacy. Our Privacy Policy is available online at www.ReaderService.com or upon request from the Reader Service.

We make a portion of our mailing list available to reputable third parties that offer products we believe may interest you. If you prefer that we not exchange your name with third parties, or if you wish to clarify or modify your communication preferences, please visit us at www.ReaderService.com/consumerschoice or write to us at Reader Service Preference Service, P.O. Box 9062, Buffalo, NY 14269. Include your complete name and address.

HBI1B

Looking for a great Western read?

Harlequin Books has just the thing!

A Cowboy for Every Mood

Look for the Stetson flash
on all Western titles this summer!

Pick up a cowboy book
by some of your favorite authors:

Vicki Lewis Thompson
B.J. Daniels
Patricia Thayer
Cathy McDavid

And many more…

Available wherever books are sold.

Saddle up with Harlequin® and visit
www.Harlequin.com

New York Times *and* USA TODAY *bestselling author Vicki Lewis Thompson returns with yet another irresistible cowpoke! Meet Mathew Tredway—cowboy, horse whisperer and honorary Son of Chance.*

Read on for a sneak peek from the bestselling miniseries
SONS OF CHANCE:

LEAD ME HOME
Available July 2012 only from Harlequin® Blaze™.

As MATTHEW RETURNED to the corral and Houdini, the taste of Aurelia's mouth was on his lips and her scent clung to his clothes. He'd briefly satisfied the craving growing within him, and like a light snack before a meal, it would have to do.

When he'd first walked into the kitchen, his mind had been occupied with the challenge of training Houdini. He'd thought his concentration would hold long enough to get some carrots, ask about the corn bread and leave before succumbing to Aurelia's appeal. He'd miscalculated. Within a very short time, desire had claimed every brain cell.

Although seducing her this morning was out of the question, his libido had demanded some sort of satisfaction. He'd tried to deny that urge and had nearly made it out of the house. Apparently his willpower was no match for the temptation of Aurelia's mouth, though, and he'd turned around.

If he'd ever felt this kind of desperate need for a woman, he couldn't recall it. During the night, as he'd lain in his narrow bunk listening to the cowhands snore, he'd searched for an explanation as to why Aurelia affected him this way. Sometime in the early-morning hours he'd come up with the answer. After years of dating women who were rolling stones like he was, he'd developed an itch for a hearth-and-home kind of woman. Aurelia, with her cooking skills and voluptuous body, could give him that.

With luck, once he'd scratched this particular itch, he'd be fine again. He certainly hoped so, because he had no intention of giving up his career, and travel was a built-in requirement. Plus he liked to travel and had no real desire to stay in one spot and become domesticated.

Tonight he'd say all that to Aurelia, because he didn't want her going into this with any illusions about permanence. He figured that when the right guy came along, she'd get married and have kids.

Too bad that guy wouldn't be him….

Will Aurelia be the one to corral this cowboy for good?
Find out in: LEAD ME HOME

Available July 2012
wherever Harlequin® Blaze™ books are sold.

This summer, celebrate everything Western
with Harlequin® Books!

www.Harlequin.com/Western

HBEXP0712

Harlequin® Blaze™

red-hot reads

Three men dare to live up to naughty reputations....

Leslie Kelly

Janelle Denison and Julie Leto

bring you a collection of steamy stories in

THE GUY MOST LIKELY TO...

Underneath It All

When Seth Crowder goes back for his ten-year high school reunion, he's hoping he'll finally get a chance with the one girl he ever loved. Lauren DeSantos has convinced herself she is over him...but Seth isn't going to let her walk away again.

Can't Get You Out of My Head

In high school, cheerleader Ali Seaver had the hots for computer nerd Will Beckman but stayed away in fear of her reputation. Now, ten years later, she's ready to take a chance and go for what she's always wanted.

A Moment Like This

For successful party planner Erica Holt, organizing her high school reunion provides no challenge—until sexy Scott Ripley checks "yes" on his RSVP, revving Erica's sex drive to its peak.

Available July wherever books are sold.

HB79698

Harlequin Super Romance

Debut author

Kathy Altman

takes you on a moving journey
of forgiveness and second chances.

One year after losing her husband in Afghanistan,
Parker Dean finds Corporal Reid Macfarland at her
door with a heartfelt confession and a promise to save
her family business. Although Reid is the last person
Parker should trust her livelihood to, she finds herself
captivated by his silent courage. Together,
can they learn to forgive and love again?

The Other Soldier

Available July 2012 wherever books are sold.

This summer, celebrate everything Western
with Harlequin® Books!

www.Harlequin.com/Western

HSR71790